Forbidden Frontier

CHRISTIE HARRIS

Forbidden
Frontier

Drawings by E. Carey Kenney

ATHENEUM   New York   1968

To my family, the Irwins
who homesteaded in this Shuswap Indian
country during my early childhood

PART I

"Rebellion, the secular will not to surrender . . . keeps us always erect in the savage, formless movement of history.

". . . rebellion puts total freedom up for trial. It specifically attacks the unlimited power that authorizes a superior to violate the FORBIDDEN FRONTIER."

The Rebel, by Albert Camus.

1

SHE WAS NINE THE DAY IT ALL BEGAN. HER WORLD WAS still the lovely, well-ordered world of the Hudson's Bay Company's far western department. And it was the kind of day she loved, sunny yet brisk, with the whole of Fort Alexandria astir.

From a favorite spot by the log palisades, she glanced eagerly up the Fraser River. At any moment she might catch the first strains of the canoe song heralding the boats. They would come out of the north with the year's fur from the lakes and forests of New Caledonia. Or she might hear first the skirl of bagpipes from the south leading a column of horses up from the dry, open ranges of Fort Kamloops.

They met at Alexandria each spring: the beribboned boatmen and the red-shirted packers. They met with loud jokes and laughter and with the pride of the Fur Brigade.

3

Her father, Chief Trader at the Fort, was ready for them. His shirt was dazzlingly white against the black of his frock coat. His tall hat shone, beaver. He was Lord of the Wilderness around him; and Alison caught her breath, thinking ahead to his glorious moment.

As soon as the men had been regaled in celebration and the furs had been transferred from boats to pack horses, he would lead the Brigade south. Riding out of the Fort on his big blue roan, preceded by his two hunters and followed by his piper in full Highland regalia, he would raise his hat as the cannon boomed a salute in his honor. Alison would watch proudly, the Scottish blood in her own veins dancing to *The March of the Clans* that the piper would be playing.

"Alison!" her father called, startling her.

"Yes, Father."

His eyes swept her tousled braids, her smudged deerskin shift, her bare feet.

"Yes, Father," she said again, in reply to his unspoken order. And she raced in through the gates and on into their family quarters to make herself presentable, as the daughter of the Chief Trader should be on a Company occasion.

Her mother, already dressed in new, fringed deerskin, was standing in front of the long mirror adjusting her canoe-hat. A native of a faraway island near Alaska, Djaada (Djā′ada) was taller and fairer-skinned than the Indians of this dry inland country; and she wore the identifying totems of the Coast tribes: Raven was painted on her canoe-hat; Killer Whale glinted from silver bracelets and earrings.

Gliding to a small, totem-carved chest, Djaada spoke softly in her native tongue. "Today you will wear the gold bracelet." She gave a happy cry as she took out the heirloom. Then, "For you!" she announced proudly, holding out a flattened circlet of gold that had been exquisitely decorated in a Haida (Hy-dah) Raven design.

"For always?" Alison asked, scarcely daring to touch it.

"For always." Her mother smiled at her before turning to gaze out the window. She wasn't seeing palisades, the girl knew; she was seeing a fleet of brilliantly-painted high-prowed canoes slicing through sea swells towards a totem pole village, towards the great occasion where as a girl she herself had first worn the bracelet. "We must go home soon, you and I," she murmured.

"Home? But —"

The Fort bell clanged. The cannon boomed.

"They're coming!" the girl screeched, darting towards the door.

"Alison!"

"Yes, Mother." She knew. A girl with Haida chiefs' blood did not appear disheveled on a great occasion. She yanked off her smudged dress.

"Alison . . . Alison . . ." Djaada seemed to be turning the word over and over on her tongue. "Alison." As if it had a strangeness not altogether pleasing.

But there was no time to think of that now. The great occasion had started.

The horses came first. The lovely, lovely horses! Wild

5

yet tractable, as only Indians could make them.

The furs arrived with a streaming of Company banners, a flourish of red paddles, and a hubbub of voices. A discharge of firearms and a clamor of children and dogs gave way very soon to a scraping of fiddles. The *regale* was on. And the Chief Trader's daughter watched it in silent enchantment.

Mountains of precisely-pressed ninety-pound fur pieces were handled at Fort Alexandria.

Five skins, however, had not been baled. "Silver black fox!" Djaada murmured, stroking lustrous pelts. "And sable! Almost as perfect as sea-otter." Then she turned to the fifth skin, a white beaver. "Fit for a Head Chief," she said, reverently touching it. Her eyes lit as the Chief Trader approached. "I must have these five skins," she said eagerly to him.

His eyebrows shot up in surprise. "Those skins are the property of the Company, as you well know." His Scots tongue put a burr on each *r* sound. "We'll have them baled safe in no time."

"But —"

"There are no buts, my dear, and no exceptions whatever. The Crown granted every fur in the land to the Hudson's Bay Company."

"Perhaps the Crown granted what the Crown had not the right to grant," she retorted in slow, accented English.

He seemed astonished at her outburst. "Every fur goes to London," he said, closing the subject before he turned to stride away from them.

An aristocrat did not beg; but Djaada's eyes flashed.

Her lips closed in a thin line.

"You wanted the furs for our gift chest," Alison suggested sympathetically.

Djaada answered with quiet ferocity. "We are a great family, and our gifts must be worthy of us at the potlatch."

"I know, Mother. But we have lovely things already in the gift chest."

Her mother dismissed mere beaded deerskin and lengths of cotton cloth with a wave. "We have nothing really worthy of such an occasion, the occasion when you receive your proper name."

"Mother," Alison said, "Alison is a —"

"A foreign name! A name that belongs to your father's clan, not ours; not yours and mine."

"But —" She knew how it was, though. In her mother's coast tribe, a child belonged to her mother's clan and not to her father's; she wore the identifying totems and the traditional names of her mother's people, not her father's. In her mother's eyes, Alison knew that she was highborn Haida Indian and not Scottish at all. So she must receive one of the high-ranking Haida names. She must receive it ceremonially at a potlatch, and the important witnesses must be presented with gifts after the ceremony, gifts worthy of the noble family that gave them.

The five pelts would have been suitable gifts.

Alison Stewart sighed.

"If only we had coins to give!" Djaada said. She looked at the bracelet her daughter wore. It had been fashioned from gold coins spent by Boston traders in Alaska.

7

Djaada now had no contact with Boston traders. Fort Alexandria was inland, and Boston traders never came up this river.

Mother and daughter sighed. Then they saw Mr. Stewart hurrying back to them.

"Great news!" he announced. "A friend of mine, Archibald Sutherland, has been posted to Kamloops; and he's brought a bride with him. Jeannie!"

"Jeannie!" Alison knew who she was — the daughter of a fur trader in the north. She had red hair, an unusual thing for a girl in the Indian Territory west of the Rockies. "We'll see her red hair."

"Aye, you will," her father agreed. "Sooner than you think. She's invited you to Kamloops. You and your mother will go that far with the Brigade and stay there till I come back."

"Father! You mean *we're* going out with the Brigade?"

"You are. So you'd better skedaddle, the two of you, and prepare for the journey."

Alison raced for the house. Then she waited for her mother who moved with the slow grace of a highborn Haida.

"I will walk to Kamloops," Djaada stated when they had reached their quarters.

Alison opened her mouth to protest. She closed it in understanding. On that faraway island her mother had never seen a horse. She had grown up learning the skills of the sea. And now, in her fierce Haida pride, she would do nothing she could not do expertly. She would not shame herself with awkwardness. It was why she had never accompanied the Brigade south, like other wives.

"I'll walk with you," the girl offered.

"No. You will ride."

Alison had ridden all her life and had her own pony, Raven. Under Djaada's direction, her slave had worked the Raven totem design in beads for his browband, so that he would be marked with the proper crest. Alison must always be visibly identified as one of the Haida.

Her father often frowned at her totems. Still, they meant so much to her mother!

Alison was excited about going to Kamloops. Once it had been the connecting link between the Company's two vast areas of operation west of the Rockies: *New Caledonia* that reached north to Alaska, and the *Columbia District* that stretched south to California. It had maintained two thousand horses for the Brigades that wound south to the Columbia River through the easy, open Okanogan Valley. Now, with most of the Columbia District lost to the Americans, Kamloops was a smaller establishment. Brigades were smaller, too; and they had to make their way south from Kamloops through the Cascade Mountains to posts on the lower Fraser River. Nevertheless, moving off to Kamloops was exciting for Alison; especially as she rode ahead with the gentlemen, a-tinkle with bells as befitted the Chief Trader's daughter.

Her excitement mounted as they neared Fort Kamloops after two weeks on the trail. Finally she caught the distant salute of the cannon; and when the answering bagpipes skirled at the head of the column, her heart was as

Highland as her father's.

Mr. MacNeil, Chief Trader at Kamloops, was waiting for them in his frock coat and beaver hat. He welcomed Mr. Stewart with all the formal courtesies due to the Captain of the Fur Brigade. And he bowed perfunctorily to Djaada and Alison. Then with obvious delight he led out a young lady with red hair. "The bride, Mrs. Archibald Sutherland," he said grandly.

"Jeannie!" Mr. Stewart held her off with both hands before he kissed her cheek fondly. "Dear lassie, you're a sight for sore eyes!"

"Would you ever suspect there was a drop of Indian blood in her veins?" Mr. MacNeil demanded with evident satisfaction.

It wasn't just the red hair, Alison realized as she watched the bride shyly. The difference was in her speech too, in the way she addressed the men and in the way they spoke to her. And her clothes! Dove gray silk fell in shining folds to her moccasins. A big silver-and-amethyst thistle was pinned into soft lace at her throat; the thistle, Alison knew, was a Scottish *totem*. Jeannie must belong to her father's tribe. She remembered hearing that Jeannie's Indian mother had died young; that she'd grown up close to her father; and that her father's family had sent letters, books, and dresses on the Company vessels.

It might be nice to be Scottish, she thought. Then catching her mother's eye, she flushed. It was nicer to be Haida, especially if you ever got a chance to see the totem pole villages and the canoes that braved the seas from Alaska to California.

"And this is Djaada," Jeannie was saying, "and wee Alison." She smiled warmly at them. "Away in out of the hot sun!" she invited.

"We've a lady at the Fort now, Mr. Stewart," Mr. MacNeil said before casually indicating a hovering Indian woman in a red, Company-cotton shift. "The squaw will show you your quarters, Djaada," he said, and turned instantly back to Mr. Stewart. "Wait till you taste Jeannie's tea scones! You'll be wanting her to teach your daughter."

Alison gave a small start. Was that why she had been brought? To learn to not be so Indian? She recalled the wistfulness in her father's voice when he had told her about the daughters at Fort Vancouver and Fort Victoria. They dressed in stomachers and fine lace for Company occasions. They even went to school faraway. Away east of the Rockies!

"Just follow Red Feather," Jeannie urged them as the Indian woman glided off followed by several small children.

She had a red feather worked in tiny beads on her moccasins. And the quarters she showed them were the customary HBC quarters: beds with good rope springs, scrubbed floorboards with furs laid on them, candles in wrought-iron wall-brackets.

It was Mr. MacNeil's sittingroom that fascinated Alison when she sneaked in behind her father. He must have had things packed in! There was a graceful red velvet chair, a dark blue rug below it, and above it a painting such as she had never seen. It pictured a golden-haired lady in a wispy white dress with a sash as red as the chair. It occurred to Alison that a lady so strangely pale might well be the ghost of some young woman like Jeannie.

Jeannie was also in the sittingroom, with the men! An incredible departure from custom as Alison knew it. She was pouring tea and smiling at the praise they were heaping on her scones. And when she noticed Alison, she beckoned to her, holding out the plate of scones.

Alison shook her head, which was foolish because she did want to taste them.

Jeannie's husband seemed entranced by the portrait. "A bonnie painting, Mr. MacNeil," he commented.

"My wife, Margaret," Mr. MacNeil answered. "She died when our son was born." He was silent for some moments. "I left the boy with my family and joined the Company. I've not seen him since." He picked up the framed miniature of a fair-haired boy. "He's named Fergus like my father. We Scots are great ones for keeping up the old family names."

Like the Haida, Alison thought.

"A bonnie lad, Fergus," Jeannie observed, passing the miniature on to her husband before she took the plate of scones to Mr. Stewart. "Do have another," she coaxed him.

"It's like home," he said, taking one. Her father said *home* the way her mother said *home* about the totem pole village.

"A woman pouring tea at a tea tray," he went on in that same, strange, wistful way.

A white woman, he meant. Until that very moment, Alison had thought only in terms of white men. Now, suddenly, she realized that there were white women as well as white men. Whole families of white people! It was a startling realization.

In the days that followed, Alison looked at the portrait again and again. And she watched Jeannie. Whole families of white people! But there was little time to really consider the matter. There were too many other things to do.

There were many bustling, crowded days before her father left with the combined New Caledonia and Thompson River Brigades. Alison found them exciting, especially when she watched the boy Ross.

Ross was very good-looking. His smile was as lively as his dark eyes. Though he couldn't be more than eleven, he seemed very involved in getting the Brigade off on the next leg of its journey. He moved horses, often standing on his own mount's bare back. He shot back and forth across the river with messages, leaving and arriving with a flying leap.

"Your name's Ross," Alison said finally as the Brigade was disappearing.

"I know." He gave her a friendly grin. "It's a Scottish name."

"So is my name. Alison. At least that's my name now until I get my real name."

"Real name?"

"My Haida name. I'm Haida. I suppose you are Shuswap." The Indians around Kamloops were Shuswap.

"No. I'm a Scot." He was positive about it.

"Oh." She knew that lots of tribes let you belong to your father's people; but she explained how it was with her Coast tribe.

"Mr. MacNeil's my father," Ross said.

"Mr. MacNeil?" Instantly the portrait of Margaret jumped back into her head. "Have you ever seen a white woman?" she blurted out.

"No. And I don't want to."

"You don't want to?"

"No." He flushed, just a little.

"But her golden hair's pretty."

"Want to see something golden that *is* pretty?" He opened a small buckskin bag that hung on his chest. He poured out gold nuggets. "Here. Take them!"

Alison took them with joyful squeals.

"Tomaah and I find lots of gold," he informed her. His cousin Tomaah was a chief's son. "We find nuggets in the creeks. Like the men in California."

"I wish I did because . . ." Her voice faded, then grew strong again, "because maybe gold nuggets could be made into bracelets for chiefs' gifts." She told him about the gift chest and the coming ceremony. "It means so much to my mother to have me given my rightful, high-ranking Haida name," she said.

"Hey! You're a highborn lady . . . with a birthright. Like the maidens in the stories," he explained. Kamloops had Sir Walter Scott's books in its library and Ross obviously had devoured them as Alison's father had at home. "You're a highborn lady."

15

Alison agreed. "Yes! Like Ellen in *The Lady of the Lake*." Her father had read it aloud, twice.

Ross had read it four times. And now he regarded her with lively speculation, as if she were Ellen. Suddenly he began slashing the air with an invisible broadsword. "We'll get gold for you," he offered eagerly. "Me and Tomaah. Here he comes now, with my mother."

A tall Indian boy was approaching with Red Feather and one of her children.

"Oh, she's your mother?" She liked gentle Red Feather.

It was only later, after she was in bed that night in fact, that another thought struck her. Mr. MacNeil had said "the squaw" in a very different voice from the one he had used for "my wife, Margaret." It was as if . . . as if . . . Well! As if white women were chieftainesses; while Indian women were common people.

It bothered Alison, for five minutes. Then she began thinking about herself again.

"Highborn lady." She kept whispering the words during the ensuing weeks. And now she felt a whole new excitement about filling the gift chest for the great occasion. Now a name was a romantic birthright.

"I suppose Ross is an old family name," she remarked shyly to Mr. MacNeil when she found herself standing near him by the horse corral one day.

"Family name? No."

"But —" He had said the Scots were great ones for keeping up the old family names, hadn't he?

"I've given the boy a lucky name. Mr. Ross, an Astorian, was the first fur trader at Kamloops. He got twenty prime beaver for his last yard of cotton."

Then it struck her. Of course! Ross wouldn't get his real name until his Scots clan could present it to him properly at a potlatch. "He's a wonderful horseman!" she said, watching him and Tomaah.

"Aye, the lad can handle a horse. A Shuswap seems to be born knowing how. A sixth sense, I've no doubt, like all the wild creatures."

A Shuswap? Mr. MacNeil must think she was talking about Tomaah. Well, Tomaah was a good horseman too, leaping on and off at a canter. He had more time to practice riding tricks. He didn't have to learn arithmetic and history like furtraders' children, or for that matter didn't spend time reading Sir Walter Scott.

2

ONE AFTERNOON THE HEAT DROVE ALISON, HER mother, and Ross to the river.

"It was so cool at home," Djaada murmured by and by; and her voice carried a longing that even roused Ross from his book. "So cool . . . with the wind blowing in from the sea." She sighed deeply. "And so beautiful out on the water."

"Go out on the water here!" her daughter urged her.

"In those canoes?" Djaada was instantly scandalized, and as instantly contrite.

Ross waved aside her apologies. "The Shuswaps are no great canoemakers," he admitted with a rueful grimace at the graceless, clumsy dugouts. "Wish I could see Haida canoes! Hey! Maybe . . . maybe I could go with you to the totem pole village?"

"Oh, Ross! Maybe you could." Alison was ecstatic.

She turned eagerly to her mother. "Couldn't we go soon? I told you about Ross finding nuggets in the creeks. Couldn't we give nuggets to the chiefs? For them to make into bracelets."

Djaada's eyes lighted for a moment before they narrowed in thought. "Nuggets aren't like coins," she observed finally. "Giving nuggets would be like giving mountain-goat-horns instead of beautifully carved horn spoons." Another objection occurred to her. "Nuggets may not even hammer out the way coins do." She fingered her bracelets. "Coins have a known value, like canoes and Chilkat blankets."

It was the old thing, the pride of the lordly Haida. They had to have gifts worthy of the noble family that gave them. Alison turned anxiously to the boy, her eyes pleading for understanding. "If the gold just came in coins!" she said wistfully to him.

"The gold could come in coins," he reported two days later when he met her in the stockade. He had heard his father and Mr. Sutherland talking about the new mint at San Francisco, where the Company's ship went on business.

Alison whooped in delight. All their troubles were over.

"Sh!" He glared at her and glanced about them. "Look!" he ordered. "Don't talk about collecting the gold for your gift chest nor about needing coins instead of nuggets!"

"Why not?"

He flushed a little. "It's an Indian reason, isn't it?

19

Some people don't like Indian reasons."

She knew he meant his father.

"We'll just collect the gold; then, by and by, we'll say we want it changed into coins. We don't have to say why, do we?"

"No."

"Then promise not to talk to anyone. Not even your mother."

"But — All right. I promise."

She dropped her voice to a whisper. "This is an Indian reason too, I guess; but if you give me nuggets, I have to give you something." An Indian would be shamed by indebtedness to someone.

Ross grinned at her. "Why do you think I offered the nuggets in the first place? You're learning to make cakes, aren't you? And Scotch shortbread like Jeannie's."

"Yes!" And from that moment, Alison Stewart was wild about her cooking lessons. She waived her mother's protests about the heat of the kitchen. "Father would enjoy Scottish cakes with his tea," she countered, blushing only very slightly.

The days raced by, and she had turned ten before the cannon boomed in salute for the returning Brigade, bringing tradesgoods for Thompson River and New Caledonia. Then Alison rode home with a bundle of Jeannie's books tied to Raven's saddle. One was a treasured cookbook.

When snow whitened the world at Alexandria, Alison went out on snowshoes. On some days she carried a rifle, and Indians raised their eyebrows. Women were not hunters.

Her father insisted that she shoot well, and that she read well. "Sound your *r*'s, lassie!" he commanded. "A Scot puts a ring on them."

"But a Haida doesn't," she protested once. Her mother couldn't manage an *r* at all; there was none in the Haida language.

"What a Haida does is neither here nor there," he told her with unexpected brusqueness. "A Stewart's a Scot, lassie. And don't you forget it!"

"But —" She wasn't a Stewart. Not really. She wasn't Scottish like her friend Ross. Still, not liking to disappoint her father, she put a hearty ring on every *r* in *Young Lochinvar:*

Oh, young Lochinvarrr is come out of the west.
Thrrough all the wide Borrderrr his steed was the best.

There was plenty of time to practice *r*'s in the long, long cold winter. There was plenty of time too for thinking about the raw gold that would be turned into gold coins for the potlatch, where her mother would undoubtedly give Ross something very fine, like a slave, in return.

One evening while her father was away as usual, playing chess or conversing with the gentlemen, Alison sat dreaming over a book in their family quarters, until a deep sigh from her mother made her glance up.

"It's so quiet here!" Djaada said almost desperately. "At home . . . At home there's singing and dancing and storytelling in the winter . . . with the great fire blazing

21

up in the middle of the big cedar house . . . and hundreds of people, men and women, talking and laughing."

"We'll go home soon," her daughter promised her. She was wild to tell her about the mint in San Francisco; but Ross had made her promise.

It was Ross himself who confided in Djaada the following summer when Mr. Stewart's family returned to Fort Kamloops for a visit. He showed her two pint bottles that were half-filled with raw gold.

"Just some of it's mine — I mean ours," he told her. "Tomaah always sees something he wants, so his gold goes to the Company like the other Indians." To exonerate his cousin he added, "Indians are so poor!"

"Indians are poor now," Djaada said with spirit. "They're so poor here that if the salmon run fails, they'll die of starvation."

"Well, not the ones who are bringing in gold. Mr. Sutherland weighs mine and keeps a record of it. I have twenty-nine ounces: half for you and half for me."

"Well, you haven't had half of twenty-nine ounces of cake yet," Alison announced, handing him a basket.

"There's more than twenty-nine pounds here," he teased her, pretending it yanked his arm down. His eyes returned to the raw gold. "That's nearly twelve twenty-dollar gold pieces for you."

"Oh, Ross!" Alison sang out.

Djaada's eyes sparkled. She would give him something very very fine, her daughter knew. Maybe two slaves!

22

"We'll get tons more," he promised.

Burning with gold fever he and Tomaah rode to Alexandria with the outfits; then, striking off close to the Cariboo Mountains on their way home alone, they found a bonanza on Horsefly Creek.

Mr. Sutherland added the new gold to the old with clucks of admiration. "You'll be paying your own way to the Edinburgh University, laddie," he predicted. "And dressing like a duke, forbye."

Ross grinned as he took an arrogant stance. "Like MacNeil of Barra," he suggested, recalling a clan legend. "I'll stride out to my battlements after dinner; I'll have them sound the trumpets. *'Hear, O ye people, and listen, O ye nations. The great MacNeil of Barra, having finished his meal, the princes of the earth may dine.'* "

Blushing with embarrassment, he turned back to the raw gold. He made his voice very casual. "In the meantime, Mr. Sutherland, that's a lot of gold to have sitting around, useless. Turned into coins, sir, at the mint in San Francisco . . ."

"Aye," the trader agreed. And he in turn pointed out the same fact to Fort Kamloops' Chief Trader.

"We've about eight hundred ounces of gold altogether, now, sir," he observed later that day. "Worth nearly thirteen thousand dollars."

"Indeed!" Mr. MacNeil frowned at it.

"Young Ross here has been after me to have his share of it converted into coins, sir."

Mr. MacNeil transferred his frown from the gold to his son. "That's risky. If the California diggers got wind

23

of gold here, they'd be over us like a snowslide."

"Would they need to get wind of it, sir?" Mr. Sutherland asked him. "Could a man not do his business discreetly in San Francisco?"

"That's for the Chief Factor at Victoria to decide," Mr. MacNeil declared. "We don't want a gold rush here, wiping us out of business."

Mr. James Douglas, Chief Factor of the far western department, decided that a man might indeed do his business discreetly in San Francisco. How else did a Company man ever do his business?

"But mind now!" he cautioned the purser of the *Otter* as he entrusted him with the raw gold. "Not the least slip of the tongue in yon nest of gold diggers! Or it's the end of the fur trade."

It was not the disciplined member of *The Honourable Company of Adventurers of England Trading into Hudson's Bay* who made the slip of the tongue when he reached San Francisco in February, 1858, in the Company's steamer *Otter*. It was a San Franciscan.

"Boys!" a man from the mint said to his friend in the volunteer fire brigade, "I'll wager the next strike is going to be made up north on the Fraser River. The *Otter* brought in gold. Coarse gold and nuggets!"

Gold! Gold up north! Gold on the Fraser River!

The news whipped through the city. It raced out to the diggings where the rich placers of California were playing out:

Farewell, old California, I'm going far away,

*Where gold is found more plenty, in larger lumps, they
    say.*

Booted, bearded, and young, restless Forty-niners
headed a thousand miles north before the best claims
could be staked.

Oh, I'm going to Caledonia. That's the place for me.
*I'm going to the Fraser River with the washbowl on my
    knee.*

The Cariboo Gold Rush had started.

Living hundreds of miles up river, Alison did not hear
about it until the Brigade horses arrived from Kamloops
at the beginning of May.

Ross was with the horses. "Hey! Highborn Lady!"
he greeted her full of news. "The Californians are swarm-
ing up the river below the big canyon. So there's sure to
be war." He slashed the air with an invisible broadsword.

Alison was aghast. "Not . . . . war between white men
and Indians!" That didn't happen in Hudson's Bay country where the two were firmly allied by marriage. She
knew it was different in the American territories, of
course, but — "Not war, Ross!" she protested.

"Sure! War!" He flexed his wrist with an imaginary
rapier. "There's always war between Yankees and Indians." Having local Shuswap relatives, his ear was closer
to the moccasin telegraph than hers. "Miners ruin the
rivers for the fish. Why, the salmon may never come up
the canyon again. They may be too alarmed already."

"That would mean starvation."

"Sure! So the tribes are going to chase the miners off

25

the river . . . WHT . . . WHT." His invisible arrows shot them.

An awful thought hit her. "Ross! Was it our gold? Our wanting coins for the gift chest?"

"I suppose so." Even he looked abashed at the thought.

"Let's . . . Let's not mention them, Ross." She was overwhelmed by her own involvement in what was happening. And her father was scowling enough as it was.

"It's the end of the fur trade," she had heard him mutter to someone. "And likely the end of the British on the Pacific." His scowl had seemed to deepen. "Now we'll lose this territory the way we lost Oregon."

"Father," she ventured to ask him later, "is . . . is it really the end of the fur trade?" She felt horribly guilty. "And the end of the British?"

"It's not the end of the British," he answered with spirit. "Mr. Douglas is not helpless." Part of the Pacific Fleet of the Royal Navy was stationed near Victoria, he pointed out. Then he looked sternly at her. "You'll go to Kamloops again this year, just as we planned; but this time you'll stay close to the stockade. You'll not ride out, not even once, Alison, without a Company man in attendance."

"I'll not, Father. I promise."

"Those . . ." He groped for words. "Those lawless miners might take you for an Indian."

"But —" She *was* an Indian.

"Mr. Douglas will have rushed the word to England,"

he told her. Yet his frown blackened.

She knew why. Her Majesty's Government in London had never shown much interest in its Far West Indian Territory. It had given up Oregon without a struggle.

Mr. Douglas was the one they must bank on.

And Mr. Douglas soon had his hands full. Everyone, even Alison, learned that quickly enough. Thirty thousand men arrived that spring from San Francisco alone, to discover that the Fraser was as fabulous as it was reported. The very wind seemed to carry word of fantastic strikes. For the miners there were only two problems: the Indians and the British. The Indians were angry that the gold was being taken without permission from them or recompense to them. And the British were determined to assert and keep the authority they had had during the trade years. Tempers ran high on all sides.

Alison waited and worried. Maybe all this was her fault. And when word came first that the Indians were killing the miners, and then that the miners were killing the Indians, she could not contain her anxiety.

"What's going to happen?" she implored her father. But even Mr. Stewart did not know. Only Mr. Douglas could act.

Word was not long in coming. Mr. Douglas had arrived at the Big Fraser Canyon, where most of the miners were, with an alert, well-armed naval escort. "You'll take no action against the Indians in British territory," he had informed the organizing miners.

"And what if we do take matters into our own hands?" the angry miners challenged.

27

Mr. Douglas had replied calmly, "Then I will cut you up into mincemeat." He indicated his bluejackets, and he obviously meant what he said. "You will not use firearms to protect your rights here because you have no rights. You are here only on sufferance."

Next it was Mr. Douglas's job to quiet the Indians. Alison followed avidly the stories that came up river.

He summoned the Chiefs and received them with ceremony. White men were as numerous as the ripples on the river, he informed them, and now that the great flow of white men had reached this land, more and more would pour in. "Who can stop a river?" he asked them.

However, the Queen would suffer no harm to come to her Indian children. She was sending her soldiers to protect their interests. Until the soldiers arrived, the Indians

must trust the men they had always trusted, the Hudson's Bay Company.

He appointed magistrates in each tribe to keep the *Queen's Peace*. He appointed Indian constables to assist each Indian magistrate, solemnly investing them with insignia, batons, and gold coins.

It was the River, however, that really kept the *Queen's Peace*. The melted snows of the entire, gigantic watershed surged through the canyon and washed the miners off the rich bars. They flooded the lower valley, with water and then mosquitoes. Disgusted, the miners vanished.

"They're gone! They're gone!" Alison squealed when the word reached Kamloops.

"They'll be back," Ross told her. "And the Indians'll

be ready for them."

"You're not an Indian," she reminded him anxiously. "Ross, you're Company. And the Company doesn't want trouble."

"And it doesn't want miners," he retorted in triumph.

The shining new coins for the gift chest failed to cheer her as they cheered her mother. Every time Djaada joyously ran her fingers through them, Alison felt guilty.

She felt guiltiest about the salmon. Maybe after the miners the salmon wouldn't come back. The Indians were worried, she knew. In fact, that was their main worry. Even for the Company, salmon was the staple. But for the Indians, life depended on the fish.

Alison and her mother stayed on at Kamloops for longer than usual, partly because of all the trouble. And Alison was caught up with Ross and Tomaah in the tribe's alarm for the salmon.

"What if they don't come?" she kept saying, wide-eyed with concern. And when Red Feather decided to take her family west along the Thompson to watch, to see, Alison begged to go with them.

Her father was away; and her mother allowed it.

Wild with concern, she kept riding ahead with Ross and Tomaah; and all along they found the people waiting. Patient as the sagebrush. Men had their nets ready. Women's hands were tensed on fishknives. All eyes watched the river.

Then the salmon came. Ruby-red sides flashed in the sun as the sockeye jumped and threshed, making their valiant way upstream against the frothing rapids.

People cheered. They hailed the fish with ancient reverence. Men dipped their nets joyfully from their age-old inherited fishing stations. Women sang as they readied the catch for drying.

"The salmon are not alarmed," Tomaah said in deep relief.

"Not yet," Ross agreed.

"The salmon are not alarmed," Alison reported to her mother.

"Not yet," said Djaada.

3

FINALLY IT WAS DECIDED, AT LEAST IN DJAADA'S AND
Alison's minds. They would go on the long planned journey the next summer. And Djaada was happy.

"We will go all the way out with the Brigade," she told
Alison. "We will go on to Victoria and take the Com-
pany's ship north. Oh, wait till you see the North Coast!
Wait till you see our state canoe, seventy feet long!
You'll be so proud to be Haida!"

Her father was not so happy.

"The world has changed, lassie," he told her one day.
"Our world, at least." He sighed before he continued.
"They've cancelled the Company's license."

"Oh no, Father!" Then it *was* the end of the fur trade.
Guilt overwhelmed her.

"Aye. We're a Crown Colony now, the Gold Colony
of British Columbia, with Mr. Douglas as Governor. He's

no longer with the Company. Governor Douglas is with the Royal Engineers, and the Police Force, and the lordly English judge who'll ride circuit in the gold camps. Aye, we've lost Mr. Douglas. And we've lost the right to exclusive trade with the Indians."

Her father's gloom dulled Alison's elation over the coming trip. Yet she did all that her mother asked, and sometimes recaptured the old excitement.

Djaada kept describing the coming Haida ceremonies, drilling her in the etiquette of the North Coast. "Hold yourself proudly!" she admonished. "Move slowly! Remember you are Haida!"

Alison did try.

"Are you all right, lassie?" her father asked her one day when she was remembering she was Haida.

"Of course, Father." She glanced inquiringly at him.

"You don't seem to be scampering about much lately."

"Well, I am growing up, Father."

"Aye." He looked speculatively at her. "Alison, no doubt they'll start a school for Colonial young ladies in Victoria. You could go out with the Brigade."

"I am going out with the Brigade, Father. I'm going to the North Coast."

He frowned at her. Later she heard angry voices: her father's and her mother's. That was something else to worry about. Why couldn't her father accept the fact that she was Haida? The trip became more and more of a worry as the winter passed over.

Then the miners arrived. Even before the new grass!

They swarmed along the river by the thousands, below and around and above Alexandria.

"Stay close to the stockade!" her father commanded.

"All summer!" her mother added fiercely.

"All summer?"

"All summer!" her father thundered. Because of the miners they weren't going to the North Coast after all. They were going just to Kamloops.

It was Tomaah's fault, Alison found out, for when the first three gold diggers of '59 had emerged from the big Fraser canyon to look speculatively along the Thompson, Tomaah had led them away from his people's river by showing them the place he and Ross had once found on Horsefly Creek. Word of this new strike had raced south through the gold camps on the lower Fraser; and now the great rush was north and east, towards the Cariboo Mountains. Kamloops was being bypassed.

Now, Oregon and Montana as well as California were emptying into the area. Men were pouring in from across the oceans. Company servants were deserting to try their hand at gold mining. Company officers were being harassed. Indian women were being molested.

Djaada accepted the need to go to Kamloops, though not happily. "Next year nothing will stop us from going home for the ceremony," she declared. "If we can't go south with the Brigade to meet the Company's ship, we will walk north and west on the old Grease Trail." This was the ancient route over which eulachan (oo-la-kan) fish oil was carried in inter-tribal trading.

When the Brigade horses arrived, Ross and Tomaah

were with them. And Tomaah was almost strutting.

"*My* father is keeping the *Queen's Peace* at Kamloops," he informed Alison and her mother.

Djaada looked at him sadly.

"That's wonderful, Tomaah!" Alison said quickly, before her mother could make one of her penetrating comments. And she changed the subject abruptly. "Ross! You have a *bonnet!*"

"Aye, lassie," he agreed with a broad grin and an even broader Scots accent. "Jeannie gie it tae me at Christmas." He swaggered gayly in it.

"And a new horse!" A big spirited black.

"Gallant Steed." He patted the glistening neck proudly. "Take a look at his browband."

It was a strip of red-beading laid over buckskin; and, centering the band was a silver thistle.

"You're not the only one with a crest to mark your possessions, Highborn Lady."

"You'll be wearing a kilt next," she teased him.

Tall and handsome, Ross was fourteen now. Alison just hated to think of all the pretty glances that must be turned on him when he galloped into an Indian encampment with his cousin Tomaah.

"Ross!" She had noticed his red shirt. "You're dressed like a packer."

"I *am* a packer." His eyes shone. "With all the men deserting, *I* am taking the Brigade south."

"Oh, Ross! How I wish —" But what was the use of wishing? *She* was going to Kamloops, to the stockade at Kamloops so that no rude gold miner would take her for a young squaw and treat her the way no daughter of the Company must be treated.

"I'll tell you all about it when I get back," he offered, tweaking one of her long, dark braids.

When he did finally return to sweltering, brown Kamloops months later, he was infuriatingly silent.

"Didn't you see *anything*?" Alison implored him. "Ross!" she demanded. "Hurry up and tell me about the gold camps! I'll be gone in a few days."

Pricked and prodded, at last he burst out with, "Do you know what a halfbreed is?"

"Well . . ." Of course she knew what a halfbreed was.

"Half white man, half Indian, and half Devil." He spat the words at her.

"Ross!" That was ridiculous. "Jeannie's not a half Devil. And I'm certainly not a half Devil."

"Well . . . maybe I am."

And that was all he would say. What could have happened?

Her father, too, was mysteriously quiet about the trip south. He had gone farther than Ross, having sailed over to Victoria to see Governor Douglas. Yet the family spent a week at Kamloops, then went home, and had been home at Alexandria for a week before he even mentioned that there had been Haidas encamped at Victoria. They had paddled all the long way down the coast in their mighty canoes.

"Haidas!" Djaada's eyes sparkled. "We could have

gone home with them for the visit. Oh! If only we had been with you! Next year we will go with you."

"We'll discuss that when next year comes," he answered. And he stalked off abruptly.

Alison had a strange, chilled feeling. Something was wrong. Something was wrong with the Haida.

She knew that her mother sensed it, too, but would not beg for information. There was a new, fierce protectiveness about the way Djaada fingered the coins in the gift chest, a new intensity about the way she previewed the coming great occasion when her daughter would finally receive her rightful, high-ranking name.

Her mother's plans were not the only ones, Alison soon decided. She often found her father watching her with appraising eyes, and she wondered what he had in mind. She thought she knew. And she was right.

"There are young ladies in Victoria," he remarked one wintry morning. "You could go to school with them."

"School?" she protested. "Father I do learn arithmetic and history and —"

"There's more to an education than books, lassie, a young lady's education. There's . . . Well, there's dressing and manners and dancing and . . ."

She longed to tell him that her mother was drilling her in dressing and manners and dancing, every evening while he was away enjoying music and conversation. She knew exactly how to break off a piece of smoked salmon, dip it into a totem-carved bowl of eulachan oil, and then wipe her fingers daintily on a shredded-cedar-bark napkin. She knew precisely how to move her feet to the drumbeats in the feast house. And she had a detailed mental picture of herself in ancient Haida regalia.

But she knew he was talking about white girls' dressing and white girls' manners and white girls' dancing. Her slim shoulders sagged. Her father just did not seem to understand that his daughter was Haida, and not Scottish like the painted Margaret that Ross so hated.

Then at last another long winter was over and spring had come. Djaada was busy packing for the long journey. And as she waited for the Brigade, Alison wondered if this year would really be the year.

Finally, the Brigade was coming! Alison slipped on her gold Raven bracelet and listened for the first strains of the canoe song out of the north, and of the bagpipes from the South.

The horses arrived, right on time. But Ross wasn't there. Was this to be the first of another series of disappointments?

"Something's happened to Ross?" she asked a packer.

"A brother," he answered, frowning.

"A *brother*?"

Ross's half-brother, Fergus MacNeil, had arrived from Scotland; though that was not really the reason Ross had stayed at Kamloops. Men had deserted from the Company's horse farm near Kamloops to such an extent that the fifteen-year-old son of the Chief Trader had had to take charge of getting the relief horses ready. He must have hundreds of fresh horses waiting in the Fort Kamloops corrals when the horses that had come to Alexandria had finished the first leg of the long Brigade journey.

"He will be going south then?" she asked hopefully, because it did look as if she and her mother would go.

"He will be going south."

"Maybe Fergus will go too."

"I hope not," said the packer.

"Oh." Alison promptly dismissed the unpromising Fergus from her mind and imagined Ross readying the Brigade horses. He would be so pleased to be in charge. Ross was Company. He cared about the clockwork schedule of the Fur Brigade as much as his father did, or her father.

But had something happened to the boats out of the north? The horses had come, but not the furs. Day after day passed; yet the boats failed to appear.

"Even paddlers have deserted," her father guessed, fuming at the delay.

This delay would throw everything else out, all along the line. Alison kept thinking of the problems delay would raise for Ross. The very first time he was in charge of the horses!

When at last the boats did arrive, woefully short of paddlers as Mr. Stewart had predicted, there was less ceremony than usual. The annual journey was so late in beginning, there was no time for any unnecessary delay. Alison was glad. She couldn't have waited a moment longer.

But when they moved into the fort, finally, everything seemed upside down. Mr. MacNeil paid only clipped perfunctory attention to the usual courtesies extended to the incoming Captain of the Fur Brigade. The horses weren't all ready. The river was rising. And Ross was evidently in trouble. Many of the horses he was supposed to have there were nowhere in sight. It wasn't like Ross. Something was wrong.

To make matters worse, Alison learned the night of their arrival that Mr. MacNeil was going to take the Brigade south himself. Mr. Stewart had to stay at Fort Kamloops.

"You mean . . . ?" Alison was incredulous. "You mean we aren't going? After all!" It was unthinkable. They had planned so long.

"I am not going. And you are not going without me. I'm in no mood to discuss the matter."

Alison went to her mother. "What about the Grease Trail?"

Djaada considered well before she decided. "I cannot shame your father by such an action when this was not his fault. We will wait until next year."

There was nothing more to be said. All Alison could do now was worry about Ross. Where was he? No one wanted to talk about him, or about the horses. What could have happened?

The river kept rising; the Fort began flooding. "We're on the wrong side of the river," Mr. MacNeil snapped. "We'll be paddling through the gates soon."

Heat and tempers grew worse daily.

And Ross did not come back.

Maybe he was hurt. Thrown from his horse near a nest of rattlesnakes. Alison scanned the hills for some sight of him. She plagued his cousins.

"He's hunting strays we have to have," was all they answered.

On June 18th she frowned as Fergus — an elegant dandy she had despised from her first glance — cantered toward the head of the column on the south bank. Most of the horses had come in at last, but Ross had not been with them.

"What's keeping that boy?" Mr. MacNeil demanded glancing at the hills once more before scowling at the horse Red Feather had readied with her eldest son's equipment. "He knows we're short of packers."

"Couldn't Fergus help pack?" Alison ventured to suggest. But she wished she hadn't spoken, the way Mr. MacNeil looked at her.

"My son is a gentleman, Alison," he said coldly.

"But —" Ross was his son, too.

The Brigade moved off. The cannon saluted. Mr. MacNeil raised his hat punctiliously.

And then, as the column stretched away, Ross cantered in from the hills leading the last stray horses. Catching the bridle from his mother, he followed the Brigade. But for her, there was not even a wave.

What could have happened? It was Ross's young cousin, Brown Bear who finally told her the whole story, as the Brigade disappeared in the distance.

Ross had had hundreds of horses corraled on both banks of the Thompson. They had milled restlessly hating the confinement. Yet the Brigade had not come. The year before, the New Caledonia Brigade had arrived on May 20th. And on May 20th Ross had been ready. But June

41

came and still the furs had not arrived.

Then, on June 4th, a messenger had come from the lower Fraser; and immediately Mr. MacNeil had announced that he would be taking the furs south himself, leaving Mr. Stewart in charge at Fort Kamloops. He would be gone at least a year, going to Scotland on private business, taking Fergus with him. There had been no mention of what Red Feather, Ross or any of his Indian family were to do in his absence. Obviously they did not matter.

At the news Ross had stuck a feather into his red headband, discarded his red shirt in the heat, and donned fringed buckskin trousers, deliberately looking like an Indian.

The next day, Brown Bear himself had reported that

a rock was menacing the corral on the south bank. "One deer's kick would have sent it down on the horses," he told Alison dramatically. It was one of those occasional boulders, settled into the slope. Spring thaw had undermined it.

"Maybe we can throw a tree in front of it for now," Ross had suggested, frowning over at the south bank. Some emergency measure had been needed, and he had rounded up a work party.

As the party left, Fergus had appeared. "Where are you going?" he had demanded, his voice a trifle thick.

"Up the slope." Ross had indicated his direction casually.

"Go with you. Couldn't possibly be more boring," Fergus had responded.

"Sure, come along," Ross had invited, generous now that his hated half-brother was leaving.

At the top of the slope, the rock had indeed been balancing as Brown Bear had reported. "Don't go near it!" Ross had snapped when Fergus reined in close to it.

"You, ordering me!" Fergus became truculent under the influence of firewater.

"I am ordering you," Ross had said calmly, explaining the problem. "Tomaah, can you get started on the tree, I'll be there in a moment," he had added.

Then as he had turned to help Tomaah and Brown Bear with the tree, he had seen Fergus put his foot to the stone, testing its balance. "Don't do that," he had shouted.

Fergus had turned and his gaze had moved from Ross' feather headdress to his Indian trousers. "What do you halfbreed bastards think you are?" He had given a defiant push.

The boulder had toppled before any of them could reach it. It started down, bounding and crashing.

"It's going to hit the corral," Ross had announced. He leaped onto his horse. So had his cousins. They all plunged wildly down the slope while Fergus struggled to untie his horse and get mounted.

Below, before they could even give a warning, the boulder had hit the corral. Fence rails went flying. Startled horses shied in terror; nervous companions panicked. Flattening their ears, the whole herd had plunged violently and blindly into the opening made by the stone. Off they had gone, toward range land and freedom.

Ross and his companions had arrived too late to save the horses, but in time to encounter Mr. MacNeil. He had been so angry and had reined in so sharply that his big black horse had pulled up on her haunches.

"Can't you even do your job?" his father had yelled at Ross, all his pent-up frustrations finding vent in one explosion. He had glared at Ross' headfeather. "In a pinch, you're a savage!" Then he had dashed off, shouting orders.

Ross had sat for a moment stunned. Then he had wheeled Gallant Steed and galloped off to the hills. He had been too proud to explain and too hurt to want to. Instead he went after the horses. They had to be brought in. He had not returned until the Brigade was ready to leave. Then, in the pinch, he was Company. He had had to help get the furs through.

Alison heard the story silently. Were all white men like that? No, her father was different, although even he didn't really understand what it was like to be an Indian. But what would happen to Ross now? What would he do?

4

"HE WILL NOT COME BACK," RED FEATHER MURMURED the evening after the brigade had departed.

"Ross?" Alison asked in alarm.

"His father."

"But —"

"He will not come back," Red Feather said again. "I will go to live with my people."

"And . . . Ross?"

"He is a man now. Fifteen."

Actually he was nearly sixteen by the time he returned with the outfits, and he was quieter than he had ever been. He scarcely spoke to Alison when she and Jeannie accompanied the Brigade to Alexandria to bring back the Stewarts' winter clothing and snowshoes to Kamloops.

"What are you going to do until your father gets back?" she finally demanded of him.

"Until my father gets back? I am going to grow old, Alison."

That was all he would say, but it was enough. Alison was frightened by the bitterness it revealed. What would happen to Ross? What could they do for him?

When they had all reached Kamloops once more, he took the horses off to their winter ranges. And that was the last anyone at the Fort saw of him until just before Christmas.

Then, Alison was snowshoeing in the sunshine near the river when she saw him striding across country. "Ross! Ross!" she hailed him, hurrying towards him. She caught him by both sleeves. "Oh Ross!" she murmured happily; and she saw the old light leap up in his dark eyes. "Jeannie said you might come."

"Jeannie knew I would come," he answered quietly. "I have something for her." He hunched a shoulder to indicate his back-pack. "It's really something for you, though. For you and your mother."

"For *us*? Oh, Ross! What is it?"

It was doeskin, she discovered when the pack was opened. Pale yellow doeskin, soft as velvet.

"Your riding habits for the trip south next summer," Jeannie explained. "I'm going to make you riding skirts."

"Jeannie!" Alison was jubilant.

"Mother is beading a *Raven* belt for you, Djaada," Ross said, pleased by their delight in his gift. "And a *Killer Whale* belt for you, Highborn Lady."

Alison smiled at the old expression.

"My gift to your mother," Djaada announced, slip-

47

ping an exquisitely worked bracelet from her arm. She held it towards Ross.

"She will be proud to wear it," he said, formally. Then he smiled. "And now at last she'll get your crests right."

Suddenly they were laughing as they had in the old days, the lovely old days before the gold rush.

Ross sniffed the air eagerly.

"Cakes!" Alison told him. "I made tons of them for you, just in case."

"Tons, eh?" he retorted.

He stayed overnight, but would not stay on for Christmas; and he shopped in the Company store, using nuggets. He left, laden like a pack horse.

"Ross!" Alison cried out, just as he was leaving. "You have a new Scottish *bonnet*."

"Aye. Jeannie gie it tae me," he said, with a flash of his old swagger.

"Don't go yet!" she pleaded. She hadn't really talked to him. Somehow, he hadn't let her. She didn't even know exactly how he was living.

When he shook his head in refusal, she caught his arm. "You will go south with us next summer?"

"I'll go south with you," he promised. "And Alison," he added, "don't expect too much!"

Of him, did he mean? She wondered as she watched him move off over the snow. Expect too much of him? Or . . . or too much of her mother's beloved Haidas?

He came again, briefly, in early spring, bringing the beaded belts and a big, golden-chestnut horse. "Best horse in the Company's herd," he assured Alison as he ran a gentle hand over the sloping, well-muscled shoulder. "Plenty of heart!"

"He's magnificent!" she agreed, approaching quietly to touch the star on his forehead. His eyes were large, his ears small and alert. Then she noticed his browband — yellow beadwork centered by a black *Killer Whale*. "Ross!" she exclaimed, pointing to it.

"Your crest, Highborn Lady."

"You mean . . . ?"

"Time you had a big, spirited mount. That's a rugged trail through the Cascades."

"Oh Ross! Mine!" He was a glorious creature.

"I named him Kalitan."

Kalitan. That meant *an arrow, shot.* "Oh, Kalitan! You're mine! You're mine! I just can't believe it." She turned to Ross in sudden dismay. "What about Raven?" He would be brokenhearted.

"He'll be better for your mother, if she'll ride. If she won't, at least she'll let Raven carry her things. She knows him."

"They love one another," Alison agreed. "Ross, she'll have to ride this time."

"Don't try to make her . . . Alison, your mother may need all her pride this summer."

"What does that mean?"

When he wouldn't say, the old uneasiness crept into her thinking again. It occurred to her that everything Ross had done was designed to stiffen their pride against . . . against what?

"This is a beautiful *Killer Whale* your mother made," she told him, running an appreciative finger along Kalitan's browband.

"I wish I had a *totem*." He sounded strangely boy-like and wistful.

"Your thistle —"

"My thistle?" he said, with a bitterness she recognized. "I'd like a native, personal crest. Something like your *Raven* and *Killer Whale*."

"Well, why not? Every *totem* had to be acquired in the first place, didn't it? By some encounter with some being. Why don't you have an encounter? And launch a new totem!"

He smiled down at her. "I might just do that."

"Oh Ross, do! Have an encounter and I'll design the totem." She loved to trace out Haida designs: *Eagle, Bear, Frog*. "I could design one for any being," she assured Ross. "As long as he has an identifying thing — like *Beaver*'s tail or *Mosquito*'s proboscis."

"How about a half-Devil, with an identifying pitch-fork?"

"Ross!"

"I'm only joking."

She knew he wasn't.

All spring Alison rode Kalitan almost daily, delighting in the smoothness of his canter. He was a glorious animal.

Ross knew horses. He had selected and trained this one just for her; and she knew he was pleased with what he had done when he looked at her in June, as the Brigade column was forming. In her pale-gold doeskin above the warmer gold of her mount, she sat proudly, sensing his thought that she truly looked like his highborn lady. She leaned forward and whispered, "You did it all, Ross."

"And now I just wish I could —" He turned abruptly away to attend to pack horses.

What was it he feared? Or was he interested in some girl in the Indian encampment? Did he "just wish" he didn't have to disappoint the girl who had always loved him?

She pushed her worries away. It was a beautiful blue-and-green morning. And she was off at last to claim her Haida birthright. She'd be fifteen in a few weeks. Old enough to marry! . . . Was Ross interested in some pretty Shuswap?

Djaada walked south, right through the Cascade Mountains; and she walked with such pride that no one urged her to mount Raven.

Alison often dismounted to walk with her; and once, passing a group of miners on the trail, she hoped Djaada did not catch one man's contemptuous, "Sure! Didn't you know? In spite of their high hats, the Company's gents are just squawmen." He spat a wad of tobacco.

She was angry. And she was even more angry when she realized that she had felt humiliated.

These were not the only leering glances they encountered on the way south; and Alison found herself more and more eager to escape into the Company's palisades on the lower Fraser River. She was thankful when they reached Fort Hope, where the furs were to be transferred to boats. Yet she was appalled with the look of Fort Hope and the gold camps around it.

It was the Indians who were so appalling. They lounged everywhere, men and women both, dirty and degraded. Drunk! Silently accepting the insolence of white men.

When Alison and Ross walked by the river, his silent fury at the looks and comments the white men gave her scared her.

"They wouldn't look at you like that if you were a white girl," he burst out once. His knuckles were white in his clenched fist.

It was not the white men but the Indians who upset her. "What's happened to them?" she implored Ross. She could not bear to see their lack of dignity. For her, that's what they had always had — if nothing else, they had dignity. Were they weak people? Inferior? The suspicion was shattering. "I'm thankful we're catching the steamer for Victoria tomorrow," she said to Ross finally. Yet, even as she said it, she despised her own weakness, in escaping.

"I wish I could go with you," Ross said; his dark eyes were anxious. "But the Company's so shorthanded."

She looked at him in dismay, suddenly realizing that he was not going all the way with them. "I might not see you again for ages." She and her mother might meet relatives and go north in Haida canoes. Or they might arrange to go north on the steamer. Who knew when they would return?

"But you will see me." He made it a promise, that

evening and also the next morning when she was boarding the steamer. "You will see me," he repeated. "I'll look after Kalitan and Raven. Keep your feather up, Highborn Lady."

"And you watch out for that totem!"

She and her mother had donned beautifully beaded deerskin shifts for the brief sea trip. As the ship steamed down river to the gulf, Djaada watched the seagulls happily. When they moved out into the sea swells, she became a woman her daughter had never known. Her gaze absorbed the sunlit waves and the blue mountains; she drank in the ocean air thirstily; and she exclaimed over every wooded island. She told ancient sea stories with a vivacity that astounded Alison.

As they moved into Victoria's harbor, her glance darted among steamers and sailing vessels until it found what it was seeking. "There!" she cried softly.

"A Haida canoe!" Alison cried out in sheer delight. It was all her mother had promised: it was gigantic, with a towering, brilliantly decorated prow; it was swift and sleek as it sliced through the water. She surged with relief. She *was* proud to be Haida. "It's magnificent!" she told her mother.

Djaada shook off a tear and stood proudly watching one of the world's most beautiful vessels, a Haida canoe. "It has not changed," she said, almost fiercely.

"We'll go to the Fort first," Mr. Stewart said as he joined them.

Alison caught the glance he bent on Djaada; it was full of pity. There was something the matter. Again un-

easiness gripped her.

Indian encampments were on the outskirts of the muddy, booming, Gold Rush city of Victoria. The family walked to them the next day, following the shoreline so that Djaada could watch for canoes bearing her own family's totems. She had a magnificent, long-cherished Chilkat blanket around her shoulders; and she fairly bubbled with excitement. Until they reached the first group.

"The whiskey trade's bad here," her husband observed.

Djaada stopped, shocked. *"Those* are Skidegate Eagles," she said, her gaze moving from a loutish group in an unkempt camp to the proud Haida totems on their canoes. "How did this happen? To Skidegate Eagles!"

"The whiskey trade."

"Then why doesn't Mr. Douglas stop the whiskey trade?" she demanded.

"He can't, Djaada."

"I thought the Company could do anything."

"The Company's no longer in command of the Indian territory."

Alison dreaded what they would find next as they moved on in silence.

"Those are Kaigani Ravens," Djaada said, apparently stunned by the sight of a group of dirty Indians wailing for their dead.

Mr. Stewart's response was gentle. "Many are killed here. The ancient feuds of the Coast break out again here when the tribes get firewater."

It was horrible. Encampment after encampment was filthy and dilapidated. Whole families sprawled in drunken stupor.

Finally there was a low, desperate moan from Djaada. "Oh no, no, no, no!" She turned and fled back along the path.

"Those are *our* Haidas?" Alison demanded of her father. She shrank from them.

"It's a sad change," he answered.

She turned on him fiercely. "How could you let her be shocked like this? Why didn't you tell her?"

"She wouldn't have believed me. She would have thought I was trying to keep you from your birthright."

Alison turned away, deeply shocked. She raced after her mother.

Djaada seemed unaware of her, and unaware of her husband when he caught up with his family. She moved like an automaton, moaning softly.

"It's like this all along the Coast," Mr. Stewart told Alison. "It's a disgrace. But how could I describe it?"

Alison was silent. There was nothing to say. And now, nothing to be. There was no pride in being Haida.

They went back to Fort Hope in time to return to Kamloops with the outfits.

"Oh, Ross!" Alison groaned when she found him with the horses.

"I know." He put his arms around her; and she burst into tears.

"She hasn't spoken since she saw them," Alison told him. "It's . . . as if she had died."

56

Djaada's spirit seemed utterly broken. She mounted Raven without one objection. She jogged northward, a pathetic figure.

"He should have told her," Alison whispered to Ross when they were camped one evening.

"She wouldn't have believed him."

"But what'll happen to her? Her pride in her family was everything."

At last Djaada spoke. "I knew . . . I knew . . . But I would not believe it."

"Why has she broken so completely?" Alison demanded of Ross. "When she always seemed so strong. What's happened to her spirit?" Had no Indian a strong spirit?

Ross echoed her own thought. "What's happened to every Indian's spirit?" He would not discuss it or anything else with her. He simply finished the Brigade journey and left the Fort the day before his seventeenth birthday. His father had not returned after the year's furlough; instead, he had made the financial arrangements Company regulations required of men when they abandoned women who were their wives by Indian rites, but not by the laws of the Colony.

Jeannie was red-eyed and angry after her parting with Ross. "How dare white men say only *their* marriage ceremony is valid?" she stormed to Alison. "How dare they humiliate other people?" She was almost accusing when she added, *"You* have legal status as a Stewart." There had been a ceremony in Victoria with the Governor officiating; an old Company man like Mr. Stewart would have been embarrassed to have anyone except another old Company man like Mr. Douglas legalize a marriage he already considered binding. "You have legal status. Ross has only money. And he cared so much!"

He had scorned Mr. MacNeil's money, Alison knew; he had left it to accumulate with his gold coins. She worried about him all winter. How were he and his family faring? She so hoped they were accepting the rations her father was sending by way of the horse farm. Yet accepting the rations would mean that pride had turned into bitter humiliation.

Storms raged inside her all winter.

Early spring brought such an inrush of miners that Company posts were depleted of some stocks. By mid-April, Kamloops was out of rice, sugar, and flour. There were only enough potatoes and wheat to seed the farm. Company gentlemen as well as Company servants had to live on beans and bacon eked out by a little fish and horse.

"If only I could have a smoke!" Mr. Stewart complained one day. They were out of tobacco.

The Indians were in a worse plight. Women begged for jobs in the Company fields so they could draw rations. Men shot their prized horses and ate them.

There was no word from Ross and his family. He did not turn up with the Brigade horses. Alison was nearly beside herself. Maybe he had married a pretty Shuswap and thrown in his lot with her people.

The weather turned sultry at the end of April. May was hot and dry.

"The fields are desperate for moisture," Mr. Stewart observed to Alison more than once. He was always out these days: inspecting the farm, checking the fur presses, riding out to the horse farm, watching for the Brigade from Alexandria. He couldn't bear Djaada's continuing silence, Alison suspected.

Only one thing seemed to be going well, the Cariboo Gold Rush. And that did little to raise her spirits. New strikes were being made along the creeks; and with them came even more problems.

"Now it's camels," Mr. Stewart informed Alison one day. "They've imported twenty-one camels to pack into the diggings." Each camel was supposed to be able to carry a thousand pounds, instead of just two ninety-pound packs like the horses.

After that, word of the camels came in almost daily. Alarmed horses plunged off the trail into timber at the first whiff of the vile-smelling beasts. Mules backed off cliffs rather than pass close to the terrifying creatures. Even stolid oxen bolted. There were protests on all sides and threats of litigation.

Then something even worse than camels arrived in the Colony, on yet another ship from San Francisco. Smallpox! It started in Victoria, where all passengers disembarked.

The Company began vaccinating. At Kamloops they were to vaccinate on June 24th, after the brigade arrived and before the trip south to the lower Fraser. When the day came, Jeannie was reminded of an old smallpox story an Indian uncle had told her. She told it for Alison, with Djaada in the room.

One of the earliest fur traders in the north, an Astorian, had shown the Indians a tiny bottle. It was filled with the spirits of Pestilence, he had told them, the spirits of Smallpox. All he had to do, if they displeased him, was to pull out the cork; and the tribes would be devastated.

"That is the white man's way," Djaada commented.

It was her first comment in months.

"That is when they should have made a stand," she finished.

Alison caught her breath and waited. Maybe her mother was coming back to life.

But there was no time for anything more, for just then her father came in to announce that it was time for his family to be vaccinated.

"I am not afraid of the spirits in the tiny bottle," Djaada told him; her look was defiant.

She would not be vaccinated. Alison could not persuade her. Jeannie didn't try to.

Astoundingly, Ross and Tomaah turned up and were vaccinated.

"Where have you been?" Alison demanded. She was so relieved to see him that her voice shrilled.

"Getting a canoe at the Coast," he answered, ignoring her real question.

It was a canoe for Djaada, a small but beautifully decorated Haida canoe. "It may get her out on the water," he suggested.

Djaada gave a cry of joy when she saw it. She ran

her hands over its sleek sides and its Killer Whale prow. She went out in it immediately in her painted Haida hat, and was a striking figure on the water.

Ross and Alison cantered along the bank, downstream, to watch her.

"She still paddles superbly," he said in surprise as the elegant little craft nosed out into Lake Kamloops. "And now she looks Haida again." He said *Haida* with such pride that Alison wanted to cry. Before she could speak, though, he had turned and moved off eastward.

She spurred Kalitan to catch him, then wheeled back to watch her mother. Djaada might need help.

When she was free to follow Ross, he had vanished.

Djaada began almost living on the water.

"It's exactly what she needed," Jeannie remarked.

Alison agreed happily. But she began worrying again in mid-July, when the first report came in of smallpox in the area.

"She has to be vaccinated," Alison insisted, in tears.

Djaada would not be vaccinated.

She went out daily in her canoe. One evening, she did not return in it.

"Something's happened." Alison joined a search party, but not the one that found her mother. Jeannie was with the one that did, and she nursed Djaada where she found her.

Djaada died of smallpox, like hundreds of Shuswaps.

Ross came when he heard about it.

"She should have let Father vaccinate her," Alison stormed at him.

He looked at her, thoughtful. "No!" he said finally. "She had to make a stand somehow. It was . . ." He searched for words and failed to find them. "Can't you see?"

"No, I can't see."

"Well, I can. Some Indian . . . sometime . . . somewhere . . . had to stop accepting the white man's way as always right. Someone had to stop being inferior before the white man. Can't you see? It isn't what they do, it's what you do. It's your acceptance of humiliation that humiliates you. If you really believed in your way, you wouldn't be humiliated."

Alison stared at him, astonished at his passion.

"Maybe . . ." He seemed excited. "Maybe it's not too late yet to stir them up to make a stand."

"You mean start an Indian war?"

"No, I don't mean start an Indian war. I mean . . ." He flung his hands up in despair. He didn't know what he meant.

After a long silence he asked her, "What's wrong with being Indian?"

"Nothing." Her answer lacked conviction.

"Then why did I want so terribly to be Scottish? Why did I let myself be so humiliated by my father and Fergus? Why did my mother accept their contempt? Your mother wouldn't be humiliated. She made a stand."

"And she died," Alison pointed out.

"She died making a stand."

"Oh, Ross!" Alison started crying.

"Hey!" he said. He squeezed her shoulders and

changed the subject. "Alison! Know what? I ran into the camels."

"The camels?" She wiped her eyes and looked at him. "And what happened?"

"Nothing. Gallant Steed wasn't startled. It was really uncanny. Or else he just can't smell. Anyway, he must be the only horse in the whole country who isn't alarmed by those confounded camels."

"Ross!" Her eyes flew wide open.

"What is it?"

"Your encounter. Your totem."

"Hey! Why not? A camel! It really *was* uncanny."

"I'll design it tonight."

"Why wait till tonight?" He pried a large flake of bark off a ponderosa pine tree. "The identifying thing's a hump — two humps," he said as he handed the flake to her.

"Oh? The way I heard it, it's the smell."

They laughed for the first time.

"His legs have to be folded under," she decreed. A moment of doubt assailed her. "You . . . you do want a camel for a totem?"

"Why not? What's the matter with a totem that can panic those bumptious miners off the trail? I can identify with it." He grinned, and she knew he had an idea that appealed to him.

Alison looked anxiously at him. He had always fancied fighting, like Sir Walter Scott's heroes. "Listen, Ross . . ."

"You listen! Do you remember the way your mother

looked at Tomaah that time he was so proud of his father's keeping the *Queen's Peace?* She was right. Why should an Indian be proud to just stand aside while his land is being plundered and his rivers being ruined?"

"But —"

"I intend to find a way to make a stand for the Indian in me. It may not be too late . . . for me, or for them. They may just need a leader."

"Well . . ." she responded uncertainly. Then she felt a surge of spirit. They — she and Ross! — could prove that it was a proud thing to be Indian. They could stand fast together. "All right, leader," she said; and her eyes shone. "I'm your first follower. My tribe's law says I'm Indian. So I'm Indian; and from now on I make a stand for the Indian in me. Good luck to us, Ross MacNeil!" She held her head high.

"MacNeil?" He looked almost offended.

"Oh? You aren't making a stand for the validity of Indian marriage?" she asked him. "And for your tribe's law which says you belong to your father's clan. You aren't going to claim your right to wear the MacNeil *bonnet?*"

He glared at her. "Ross MacNeil," he agreed fiercely. And he lifted his head, too.

It was up to them. Alison thrilled with purpose. And in the ensuing days she made her stand in every way she could.

She made too firm a stand, she finally decided, for her father put his foot down.

"You are going off to a proper school in Victoria,"

he informed her. "You are going to take your place among the young ladies of the Colony."

Alison assumed that he also meant she must marry well, like Mr. Douglas's daughters. One of them had married the new Governor of Rupertsland.

She tried both coaxing and tears. But neither budged her father. She was going to Victoria. He made arrangements for the trip south.

As a last resort, Alison sent a message to Ross by his cousin Tomaah.

Ross did not send an answer.

"Is he rousing the Indians?" she ventured to ask Tomaah.

"How could he? He is not one of us."

She seemed to hear a certain amount of contempt in the tone. And afterwards she tossed nearly all night long, worrying about it. Was Ross being rejected by his other race now? Had the Indians accepted the white man's appraisal of his status? And if so, what would that drive Ross to do? He was such a fiery person!

The next report about the camels increased her alarm over Ross. The strange beasts were officially outlawed from the Cariboo gold trails. They were to be turned loose in dry country along the Thompson. And while Indians might not regard him as an Indian; she knew Ross was Indian enough to see meaning in every happening. His totem being was outlawed. Would he, also, become an outlaw?

Wild with worry about him, she was in no mood to be packed off to a white young ladies' school at Victoria.

But her father was adamant.

Jeannie accompanied the party to Victoria to help buy clothes suitable for a Colonial Young Lady; and also, Alison suspected, to get her over the shock of meeting a schoolmistress who obviously felt she was being very charitable indeed to overlook the savage blood in the veins of her new boarder.

Alison almost welcomed the contempt, drawing strength from her own anger. Her pact with Ross was now all that she had of him. His fierce pride was all she could share now. She cherished their joint purpose.

"It's not what they do, it's what you do," she remembered him saying.

"Don't worry about me!" she told Jeannie proudly at parting. "Just remember that I'm half white man, half Indian, and half DEVIL." No white woman would make her weep. And no white girl. Ever! She would stand fast, as Ross would, proud to be Indian.

This was in early September.

In late October a letter arrived from Jeannie with infuriating tidings. A white girl had arrived at Kamloops after crossing the Great Plains and the Rockies. She and her family were living right in the Fort now. Right in her own home Fort! A whole family of white people! It seemed a personal affront.

"I hope you hate her," she said angrily to Jeannie's letter. Then she flung herself on her bed sobbing. A whole family of white people. Living right in her own home Fort.

But the sobbing stopped abruptly. She would not cry.

She would not!

Instead, she picked up her quill pen to write an answer to Jeannie. "Please try to see Ross," she pleaded in the letter. "And tell him I'll never weaken."

She tossed the quill aside soon, not feeling like writing. She gazed out at the rain, a prisoner longing for yellow bunchgrass and sagebrush and ponderosa pine trees.

Then she picked up the pen and sketched a small camel totem.

Where was Ross, at this minute? Alison yearned to see him, to touch him, to watch his dark eyes light. She longed to gallop beside him, sweeping over the rangeland.

How could she bear her prison?

PART II

5

MEGAN SCULLY ACTUALLY BEGAN HER INVASION OF
Alison's territory earlier that year of 1862 and from half
a continent away. In the spring, while the Chief Trader's
daughter was worrying about her mother and Ross at
Kamloops, the invader was looking longingly west from
Georgetown, Minnesota, on the Red River of the North.

It seemed so foolish to stay there — doomed to a lean
life, like the runt in a litter — when they could strike out
west and make a fortune. Scores of men were pouring
into town by stagecoach from the railhead at St. Paul.
They were taking the new steamer north to Fort Garry
to join a wagon train headed for the Cariboo Gold Rush.
Why shouldn't the Scullys?

Almost ready for launching, the steamship *International* was going to travel the Red River of the North
between Georgetown and the Hudson's Bay Company's

post north of the border. Her father had helped build the ship. In fact, it was the reason they were settled at Georgetown.

And it looked as if they would stay there forever. Mrs. Scully had lost patience with moving. "We'll sit tight," she decreed. "I'm not moving again, no matter how many men ride in with stardust in their eyes."

"Gold dust, Kate," Mr. Scully corrected her. "And I think we'd do better to be going off with them."

"You can just think again then," she told him. "I've no mind to go west to worse Indian trouble. Here we've only the Sioux. Out west we'd have Commanches and Apaches and Heaven knows what other murdering heathens."

"Och, Katie!" he protested. "You listen to too many yarns."

"I? I listen to too many yarns? Well now! Isn't the pot calling the kettle black this time? 'Tis you that has ears hanging out for these glorious tales of the Cariboo Gold Rush. And you don't even know where it is."

"I do, Kate." He paused to light up his clay pipe. "On the west coast there's California. North of that is Oregon and . . ."

". . . and Indian warfare!"

"And north of that is Washington Territory and . . ."

". . . and more Indian warfare!"

"And north of that again is British Columbia with the Cariboo Gold Rush right smack in the middle."

"The *far* west, it is then? The far west, where Indian warfare's that bad they've stopped wagon trains by a

Government order. And you'd take us west, Robert Hugh Scully!"

"Now you know you'd be traveling up north of the border through Hudson's Bay country where there's nothing but peaceable trading."

"But west all the same, to a land that's sure to be wilder and fiercer for bringing up children. Is it not bad enough where we are? With the Sioux looking daggers at every white person!"

"Kate, it's worse than you think, where we are." His look lost its good humor. "The Sioux have blood in their eye this time for certain. I think we should take the children away while this good chance is offering and a wagon train going. I think —"

"Myself," Mama butted in, "I'd think more of your thinking if it wasn't tied up with a fine pot of gold at the end of a rainbow."

"What's wrong with a fine pot of gold?"

"Not a thing . . . for a single young man. But a plain pot of potatoes at the end of a spade is a far better thing for a man with a family."

"Potatoes!" he scoffed. "Will you not be told, woman? There are bad rumors circling the Red River Valley."

"Do you think I've not heard them?" Her shoulders sagged. Finally! "Och, it's hard to know what would be best for the children."

Megan silently clapped her hands. The Scullys would go to the Cariboo Gold Rush. She felt certain.

They went, and in elegant company. The new Governor of Rupertsland (the vast Hudson Bay Company territory east of the Rockies) was on his way to Fort Garry with his lady, his Highland piper, and his retinue of servants. And though Gov. Dallas rode on ahead on horseback, his lady waited for the steamer, making its maiden voyage a gala occasion. She was a daughter of Gov. Douglas of British Columbia, Megan discovered; and it seemed like an omen. Someday . . . someday Megan herself would swish by in silvergray silk and a pink parasol. Someday she would smile graciously while her maids followed after.

They went just in time. As the *International* fought her way up the wilderness river to the border, Sioux warriors swept through the land behind with tomahawks and muskets. Men were scalped and murdered. Women scalped and violated. Even children were tortured. Thrust live into stoves. Butchered. In Georgetown, only the Hudson Bay post was not burned; only the Hudson Bay staff was unmolested.

"My God! . . . My God!" Mrs. Scully kept muttering,

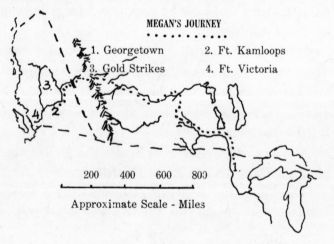

MEGAN'S JOURNEY

1. Georgetown   2. Ft. Kamloops
3. Gold Strikes   4. Ft. Victoria

200   400   600   800

Approximate Scale - Miles

clutching her children to her as the wagon train was readied near Fort Garry.

Megan looked nervously westward. "Oh, Papa!" she said, shuddering, "do you think it's safe?" Her dearest friend Prudence had been scalped. And if that could happen in Georgetown, what would the West be like?

"I think we'll be safe enough traveling in Hudson's Bay territory." He looked serious, though. He did not laugh at her fears. They were no laughing matter. "I think we'll be safe, Meg."

"If everybody obeys the rules, we'll be safe," she agreed anxiously. But even the rules were terrifying. Megan listened anxiously as they were read later in the day by the man who had been elected captain.

"NINTH: *that there shall be no trading carried on with the Indians should we meet with any parties on our way, for fear of disputes arising and getting into trouble.*"

Should we meet with any? In thousands of miles of wilderness! Megan saw the tall man in the fancy waistcoat, Mr. Fencil, rise to his feet.

"We're to starve, I suppose, Captain, instead of buying fresh meat from the natives?" *He* had wanted to be Captain.

"We'll live on what we can get from the Company posts, Mr. Fencil. We will not risk offending Indians."

"Trading would necessarily offend them, Captain? You have assured us that Indian trading is friendly in Hudson's Bay country."

"Hudson's . . . Bay . . . country!" The Captain emphasized each word. "They have the exclusive right to the

75

Indian trade. We won't risk offending them, either, since they're our only protection. Mr. Fencil, there is not one soldier to call upon in *this* Indian territory."

Not one soldier! Megan swallowed.

"TENTH: *that any person who may offend an Indian or Indians (and in case his person be demanded as satisfaction) he shall be handed over to their discretion.*"

"Hand a white man over to a savage, Captain?" Mr. Fencil sounded quite shocked.

"Better one man than a hundred!"

The Scullys were the one family in a train of a hundred and fifty gold miners. They had the only spring wagon. The others had Red River carts and saddle horses.

Mr. Fencil had three Red River carts and three tough-looking men to attend them. He rode a handsome chestnut. And as the all-wooden carts screeched westward, he flagrantly broke the rule about riding ahead. *What* if he should meet Indians first, and offend them? Megan wondered.

Megan herself was in no danger of doing that. She never ventured fifty yards from the wagon. At nights she cowered under her blanket, trying to shut her ears against the wolves . . . and against worse sounds.

There were men on watch always. One of them was eighteen-year-old Connell Moore. It was more than fear that made her stay close to Connell in the evenings. He was carefree and lively and very good-looking.

The train of carts kept screeching across the prairies, leaving each Fort reluctantly and rushing into the next Fort as if they were indeed being chased.

At Fort Edmonton, a campaign finally started to oust Mr. Fencil. Everyone had had enough of his insolence and ill temper. The climb over the Rockies was going to be by pack train on an abandoned, overgrown Company trail, bad enough without bad company. He forestalled the vote, however.

"Sorry to desert you, Captain," he said. "But nothing would induce me to go by that pass." He was taking one of the easier passes to the south, into American territory. "I'll see you in the Cariboo."

"Not if we see you first," Mrs. Scully muttered.

Leather Pass proved even worse than they had feared; but the Scullys and their group finally reached Fort Kamloops by raft with the first snows of winter. Impassable mountains had closed the way west and had forced them to turn south with the North Thompson River. The Indians, however, those few they had encountered, had appeared friendly.

"Sure, I told you we'd be safe in the Hudson's Bay country," Mr. Scully reminded his daughter. "And now you have palisades keeping you safe here."

"Thank Heaven!" breathed Megan, tattered and half-starved. Right now even she didn't want to move anymore; though most of the men went off at once to get as close as they could to the Cariboo goldfields.

With winter coming on, it was good to shelter within the Fort while Mr. Scully did carpenter work for the Company. A new post was being built on the south bank, and skilled workmen were hard to come by. The Company was glad to get one.

"I'm thankful for the old post," Megan confided to her mother. The old post was palisaded. The new one would not be. And all through the long winter, the stout log walls felt secure.

Not until spring did they seem confining.

Then, suddenly, the neat stockade seemed dingy. Unbearably dingy and stifling.

At Fort Kamloops, spring fever seemed to be gold fever, with men riding by and men even deserting the Company post for the lure of gold.

The winter was over, the memory of the hard journey only a memory. And Meg had a change of heart. Now that the trails were open, Connell would be riding north on one of them, handsomely bound for the Cariboo gold rush. Now was the time to go. Now! While there were lots of men riding that way for protection. If only they could budge Mama!

"Cariboo is one of the richest gold fields in the world," she read aloud from a previous summer's issue of *The British Columbian.* She raised her voice to be sure her mother heard her above the snip of the shears. *"On Williams Creek alone, over one hundred claims are paying from $100 to $1,000 a day to the man.* Isn't that wonderful, Mama?"

"It is," her mother calmly agreed. "Wonderful that you never tire of reading it over and over. Och, there's nothing like a spring day to show the dirt on the windows!" She sniffed with appreciation near the open door. "And nothing like the spring fields!"

"Like manure?" Megan grimaced. Then she frowned.

If they stayed here much longer, Mama would get so homesick for a farm that she'd bludgeon them along to some homestead where there'd be nothing around them but bloodcurdling coyotes and Indians. She swallowed. The Indians were friendly. But the gold rush was safer.

"Mama!" She resolutely thrust the newspaper over as undeniable proof of the sensibleness of going to the diggings. Unfortunately her mother grabbed it and read out the wrong item:

"Hundreds of men are returning every day on account of the exorbitant prices. Flour is selling for $1.05 a pound. . . . Which reminds me, young lady. It's time to punch down the bread dough . . . Flour! $1.05 a pound! And I doubt the Scullys would enjoy grazing like donkeys."

"That was last summer," Megan objected. She rolled up her sleeves and began to fight the bread dough, since she couldn't seem to get anywhere with her mother. "Things will be better this year."

"They would need to be, Meg." She turned back to the paper. *"Men should not go to the diggings without considerable means, although —"*

". . . *although,"* Megan continued triumphantly, *"Cariboo is unquestionably the richest gold field in the world. A larger percentage will succeed here than have been known to succeed in either Australia or California."*

"And in the meantime we'll at least eat if you get through with that bread."

Megan worked at the bread and she began to feel better until she happened to glance at the calico her mother had now started to cut out. It was hideous. How could any trader expect even savages to buy stuff like that? It looked like rusted barrel hoops lying on grass with fat worms wiggling through them. She hated that cloth; and at the moment she also hated old Jim, the man who had sent her ten miles of it for Christmas. Jim had been with the wagon train. "He must have been snow-blind when he bought that," she burst out.

"Well, he won't be snowblind when he comes through this spring as he promised. He's going to see the dress on you."

Megan punched at the bread dough. She put it to rise in the breadpans. And escaped.

Outside, the breeze stirred her nutmeg-colored hair, it rippled the washed-out gray of her ankle-length dress. And suddenly it lifted her spirits. She'd go down by the river. But first she'd see if there were any newspapers with new word from the gold fields.

She approached the Big House with due respect. Only the gentlemen lived there. And she rapped timidly to arouse Mr. Sutherland's attention.

"Good day to you, lassie," he said, smiling at her. "You'll be wanting a book."

"And a newspaper, if there is an old one, Mr. Sutherland."

He moved to the bookcase. And while she waited quietly for whatever he chose to hand her, she itched to tiptoe through the rooms to the Chief Trader's parlor. She had been there New Year's Day, with other Fort servants; and she hadn't been able to keep her eyes off

81

the portrait of a golden-haired lady. Undoubtedly the late Mrs. Stewart.

Mr. Stewart was impressive. Especially when he wore his Stewart tartan cloak in the winter. Lined with scarlet wool, it had a black velvet collar with huge silver fastenings. He outdid Gov. Dallas, in Megan's estimation. His lady had obviously been as elegant as the Governor's lady. He had a daughter too, somewhere. Probably an imperious daughter with billowing silk skirts and a tiny parasol. Megan sighed in pure envy.

Mr. Sutherland caught the sigh. "I'll not be long, lassie," he said briskly. He had a lovely wife also. A lady with red hair. She always smiled at the Scullys, but did not talk much to them. You came to expect that. Mr. Stewart seldom spoke to her father; when he did, he called him "Scully." Only a gentleman was "Mr." in the Hudson's Bay Company. You learned about classes when you worked for the Company.

"The Lady of the Lake," Mr. Sutherland decided.

A smile lit Megan's face. There was sure to be love in the tale of a *Lady*. She held out her hand for the welcome new story. "I'll be careful," she promised, "and not let Willie near it."

Willie was four. He had once left his teethmarks on *Hamlet*.

"Thank you, Mr. Sutherland." She hugged the book close. "Uh . . . Mr. Sutherland," she ventured, glancing through the doorway towards the parlor and the portrait, "did . . . did you know Mrs. Stewart?"

"Aye. I knew Mrs. Stewart." His tone closed the subject.

"Then . . . I mean . . . Is — ?"

"Is the book to your liking, lassie?" Though gentle, his voice forbade further probing. It was always like that when you brought up the Chief Trader's family. Had an order been issued? Was the Fort like a big, loyal family, closing its ranks against prying outsiders?

She felt her face reddening. "I'm sorry, Mr. Sutherland. I should mind my own business."

The man smiled. "You will like that book, lassie. 'Twas always a favorite with Miss Alison."

"The Chief Trader's daughter! Is . . . ? I mean . . . Thank you, Mr. Sutherland." Her embarrassed gaze sought the hand-hewn pine floorboards. A workingman's daughter should not be presumptuous.

"Miss Alison left the Fort shortly before your arrival last fall," he kindly informed her. "Soon after her mother's death. She went off to Victoria to attend a school that's been opened for Colonial young ladies." He seemed lost for a moment in fondness and sadness.

"Oh, thank you, Mr. Sutherland," Megan answered softly. "I just could not help wondering about her." Miss Alison was probably golden-haired, like her mother. And probably she wore —

A scented breeze slipped through the doorway.

"Away with you, lassie," Mr. Sutherland was saying.

"Oh! I'm sorry. I guess I was dreaming."

" 'Tis a beautiful day to dream down by the river,

provided you take a shawl with you."

"I will, and I'll dream of the trail up ahead, Mr. Sutherland."

He looked at her sharply. "You don't mean the trail to the Cariboo goldfields?"

"But we came just for that."

"So you did," he said dryly. "But you're well cared for here. And no doubt you'll have heard about Cameron's wife?"

Cameron's wife, a white woman, had ventured. *She* had returned in a lead coffin, they said, her body preserved in whiskey.

"Not much of a place for white women, the Cariboo diggings." He looked disapproving.

"The trail here wasn't much of a place, either," she reminded him. "But we made it."

"So you did," he agreed. "Well . . . away with you, lassie. Take your dreams to the river. But mind you take a shawl with you!"

"I will, Mr. Sutherland." And, forgetting all about the newspaper, she slipped out of the Big House. She darted into the Scullys' quarters to snatch up her shawl; and then, before her mother could stop her, she made fast for the palisade gate and the river beyond it. She took the book with her.

She meant to read. Instead, she thought about Connell.

He had come from Ireland, a fact that appealed to her parents. His hair was as black as her mother's, his eyes as blue as Willie's. But those blue eyes had never seen her except as someone to be helped, teased, and laughed at. She had been the subject of his silliest verses, parodies of real verses. He had not seemed to realize that a fifteen-year-old girl was practically a woman. One of these days, though, one of these days he would see her. Really see her! She hugged the book to her as she conjured up the picture.

She would be standing in a garden in a billowing blue dress . . . no, a billowing yellow dress, with a yellow parasol. Connell would ride up. He would blink with surprise at the elegant young lady. Then he'd leap down off his horse and take her face in his big hands and say —

"Have you hurted your stomach?"

She glanced down to find Willie's blue eyes fixed on her.

"Mama says you're to come right home and get 'tatoes for her. Mama says!" he repeated warningly.

A quick anger filled her.

"Mama says!"

"All right, Willie. I'll get the potatoes." She knew she had to. No daughter of Mama's would dare be caught pouting. She'd probably end up in some lonely little cabin a million miles from nowhere surrounded by six thousand acres of potatoes. Wearing gunnysack dresses.

Willie noticed the book she was holding. "I don't chew a officer's book, do I, Meg?" He looked up at his sister for reassurance. "A officer's book is more freshest than rubies." He misquoted his mother with solemn importance. "It's a pearl of great rice . . . What's a pearl of great rice? What is rubies?"

"Oh . . . just . . . jewels we'll find at the end of the rainbow," she answered, fondly tousling his hair. And her eyes sought the trail that ran west and then north to the Cariboo goldfields . . . and to billowing yellow dresses and dainty parasols.

"Mama says!" Willie warned her.

"Race you to the potatoes," she challenged Willie.

6

The spring days stayed frustrating.

Men kept riding by on the south bank, headed for the diggings.

"There won't be a claim left," Megan protested.

But you couldn't budge Mama!

"Your father has a job to finish," she said. And she went on with her sewing and then began spring cleaning. The only thing that made her sigh wistfully was the farm where the Company servants had spread manure.

"Servants!" Megan muttered fiercely. That was perhaps the biggest frustration of all, the way people, even her parents, accepted a world of gentlemen and servants.

Classes had seemed romantic on the trail the previous summer. Connell was quality, according to her parents. His family lived in a big country house in Ireland and rode thoroughbred horses.

"Maddest people you ever saw," was all Connell himself had ever said about his family; and he had said it fondly. No doubt his sisters were the kind of joyous madcap girls that Megan called, "Smarty boots! Proudy hoops!" in desperate envy.

He could have come from Ireland to the Colony the long, easy way round by steamer if he hadn't wanted to see the land. It was land that appealed to him. Megan had seen that all along. In that way he was like Mama. Only his landscape didn't have potatoes in it, it had horses prancing on it. That kind of land even Megan could enjoy. But the way to that land, she was sure, led through the Cariboo Gold Fields and money and silk dresses. If only Mama could understand! But she grew worse and worse.

It was an April morning, sunny and beautiful, when Megan almost gave up on Mama. Before Megan was even out of bed, her mother descended on her with a pair of pantalets made from the atrocious calico.

"Not squiggle drawers, too!" she said, aghast.

"Waste not, want not," said her mother. "I've made them short, Meg; no one will see them."

"But I'll know I have them on. I'll feel the worms crawling."

"Then you'll feel the worms crawling today."

"But Mama!"

"And you'll not make a poor mouth about it, either, Meg Scully."

"No, Mama." You didn't dare make a poor mouth about anything in this family. You had to look pleasant if it killed you.

"Just bear in mind that the most important thing any girl wears is the look on her face."

"Yes, Mama."

As soon as her mother had left, she jumped out of bed, stuck her tongue out at the hideous underdrawers, and then modestly dressed herself under her big flannel nightgown as she planned her escape. Something had to be done. It was time someone took measures of some kind.

With Mama on guard, it was midafternoon before she slipped out with her father's goldpan hidden under her shawl. "High time somebody in this family was learning how to use it," she muttered.

The compound that day seemed unbearably dingy and confining. Emerging from the palisades, she paused for a moment to enjoy the view. On the sage-dotted slopes, pale green bunchgrass was springing. Below, on the Company farm, stretching off to the West, newly-ploughed furrows converged, clean brown in the green landscape.

"Cattle country!" Connell had said when they had come in last autumn. A vast plateau of dry rangeland, spotted with lakes and slashed by the Thompson River. "Cattle country!" he had repeated. Then he had ridden off to see how much grass, and gold, there was in the Colony.

Megan sighed. She scanned the trails east and west. He was probably in Cariboo right now.

A small party was coming in from the west along the north bank of the river. Company men, she suspected.

There was always a lot of coming and going at the post. She glanced at the distant travelers with no special interest. She had better things to do.

A breeze gave a tug at her gray skirt, enticing her down to the river. Her gaze ranged along the nearer bank, searching for a secluded little backwater to work in. Deciding on one, she moved briskly towards it, skirting the horse corral and several thick stands of willow.

When she reached the shallow eddy, she glanced cautiously in all directions. Nobody could see her. She was well-screened on three sides by willows, and was faced on the fourth by empty green slopes beyond an empty river.

Satisfied, she kicked off her moccasins in a sudden urge of wild, delicious abandon. She laid down her shawl

and her goldpan. She felt like a colt, a lamb, a low-flying swallow. And she stuck her tongue out at decorum, and danced like a wood nymph.

Then she considered the goldpan. It was heavy, shaped like an overgrown pieplate. There should be a ritual to give it enchantment. Hm! With the flat of her hand she made three airy circles above it. Then with only a moment of shock at her daring, she gathered up her bothersome skirts and petticoats, pulling them through her legs and skewering them up with a clothespeg. Her pantalets were exposed for a few startling inches. "Worms!" she said, shuddering. Then she shrugged nonchalantly. Nobody could see her.

Now she could get down to business. Squatting square on her heels in a workmanlike manner, she grasped the

pan firmly with both hands. She practiced a half-circling motion. Your wrists had to be supple, they said, as if you were playing the fiddle. "Shake the pan, not yourself!" prospectors said.

There was a knack to gold washing; and it was high time she learned it. She scooped up a dollop of mud and pebbles. Then, tipping her pan, she let water flow in to half fill it. The trick was to wash off everything except the heavy black sand that held *color* in dust, flakes, and nuggets. Prospectors did that when they tested a creekbed. If the color gave promise of genuine pay dirt, they set up a sluicebox so they could shovel in the dirt and let the water flow through while they raked it. Heavy bits of gold if gold was there, collected between cleats nailed to the floor of the sluicebox.

She swirled . . . dipped . . . swirled . . . tipped, sloshing water with awkward persistence. Her mouth set in grim lines. It was time some Scully was shaking a goldpan after crossing those plains and those mountains and rivers to get here. Now, the Cariboo creeks were so near! Yet so far once you had lost the momentum of travel! Her weary shoulders sagged. Then they squared off again. Scoop it, then dip it, then swirl it, then tip it — with no thought for the mud that came sloshing out sideways.

"*Kla-how-ya!*" The sound startled her. She glanced round to see Connell Moore rounding the willows. He stopped dead in his tracks as he took a good look at her. "Goldpan Gertie!" he whooped out. "The Siren of the Sluicebox!" He laughed and swept off his big hat in mock admiration.

"Connell!" Megan's face lit like dawn; then it reddened like sunset. She grabbed her shawl wildly and flung it around her. "Oh, Connell! How could you?"

"You looked fine through the glasses," he blurted out, abashed himself now. "I saw you tripping this way." His face took on a brick tinge above his blue neckerchief. "I'll give you one minute." He spun about on his heel, so his back was towards her.

Frantically she yanked out the clothespeg. She shook her skirts free, covering the atrocious undergarments. If they had even been nice ones, with frills and pink ribbons. But these awful, hideous, poverty pantalets! Tears of humiliation gathered, as Connell turned back to her.

"I'm sorry I laughed," he said. "And how is the family, Meg?"

"The family? Oh . . . fine!" She swallowed her shame and looked up. Her smile broke through; and she saw him relax in the warmth of her welcome. He seemed even taller now, and broader. "Oh, Connell! I'm so glad to see you!" She held out both hands and felt his close about them. "But . . . how? . . . where? . . .why? . . ."

The old teasing sparkle leaped up in his blue eyes. "Oh . . . I heard of the Chief Trader's daughter. A beauty, they tell me."

"She's not here," Megan sang out in triumph. Then she lowered her eyes to hide a swift pang of envy. Perhaps he really had come hoping to meet a Colonial Young Lady. Like water, it seemed, people sought their own level. You learned about classes in the Hudson's Bay Company.

Still, *any* girl had her pride. And as Megan lifted her head again, a line leaped into it from the book she'd been reading:

One only passion unrevealed
With maiden pride the maid concealed.

"I'm reading *The Lady of the Lake*," she announced, quite forgetting that her thoughts had gone off at a tangent. She was curiously flustered.

Connell was disconcerted, obviously. He raised his eyebrows. He dropped her hands as though suddenly conscious of what he had been holding. He looked at her as if, in some way, she had failed him.

She felt awkwardness rise like a thorn bush between them. The old, free, comradeship of the trail was ended; and here, west of the wagons, no new one had been established. So she babbled to cover her confusion. "You know . . . *The Lady of the Lake* . . . Sir Walter Scott. Mr. Sutherland gives me books from the gentlemen's library. I've read *Hamlet* and *Romeo and Juliet* and . . ."

He was looking at her oddly. She sensed that he was disappointed. Oh, why did her tongue gallop on like an unbridled pony?

The moment passed and Connell picked up her topic. "*The Lady of the Lake,* hm?" He knocked his hat back; and paused to think. "Let me see now. How does that thing start?"

"*The stag at eve,*" she prompted.

"Of course . . .

The stag at eve had drunk his fill
Where sluiced the maid with little skill,
Where wild she swirled her goldpan round;
Nor dust, nor flakes, nor nuggets found."

"Connell!" she protested with a burst of laughter. "I didn't expect to find color here."

"Why not? The Indians found the first gold somewhere around Kamloops. So no more excuses for female ineptness! Now, if I had that pan —"

"You would use it for oats to go feeding some horse," she told him. The new awkwardness melted under the old, lively cross fire. He still wanted a little sister to tease. He would find an elegant Colonial Young Lady elsewhere when he wanted something more.

"Meg, would you care to wager that I can't produce color right here and now?"

"I would care to wager. I'll wager a . . . a clothespeg." She did not even blush as she held it towards him. "Let's see you turn up a nugget!"

"Right! . . . Show me first how you did it."

"The correct way, like this." She scooped up some pebbles to demonstrate for him.

"Now," he said, "want to see some real panning?" He He squatted and began swirling the goldpan.

Megan watched, archly raising her eyebrows. Then her gaze slid away from the goldpan. He *was* taller and broader; but his movements were as easy and graceful as ever.

"A nugget!" he sang out, reaching into the pan with

95

a triumphant "Yahoo!"

She looked into the hand he extended. "It *is* a nugget!" She blinked, unbelieving. But it still was a nugget.

"You weren't doing it right," he informed her. "I jerk harder than you on the half-circle, to toss the gold free. I jerk it more sharply towards me."

"Let me try!" She grabbed the pan from him. "Imagine! A nugget! Right here at Fort Kamloops! Jerk it sharper towards me, hm?"

"I believe you would, Meg," he said, taking the gold-pan and spilling its contents. "And get wetter than ever."

"You mean . . . ?" Understanding dawned fast. And anger. She was not a child any longer, to be teased and tormented; and Connell should know that. She confronted him fiercely. "Tomorrow I'll be —"

"Sixteen. The nugget was meant as a present." He took a small buckskin poke from his pocket and swung it before her. "I managed to get you a Williams Creek nugget as the start of your fortune."

Megan's indignation melted. "A Williams Creek nugget!" She cupped her hand reverently to receive it. "Oh Connell! I'm so pleased that I'm . . ."

"Crying?" He wiped her eyes; and then he showed her the handkerchief.

"Mud!" she yelped. "Connell! . . . am I all mucky?"

"Oh . . . just . . . all over," he assured her. Then he parodied more lines from the book:

"What though the mud had marred her frown;
Had slightly tinged her cheek with brown?"

96

"Why didn't you tell me before?" she demanded. She started scrubbing her face. "I'm so humiliated! But I'm so delighted too! A Williams Creek nugget! You're sure it's a Williams Creek nugget?"

"Look for yourself, Meg. It's blue."

"You mean different gold's different?" The nugget was bluish.

"Certainly. From the different alloys. Every creek has its special geological conditions. An expert can tell where a bit of gold came from."

"Imagine!" She dropped the Williams Creek nugget into the goldpoke, pulled the strings at the top, and then hugged her hands over the start of her fortune.

"Does it mean that much, Meg?"

"Oh, yes!" Most of all it meant that Connell had remembered her birthday. She felt his fingers close over hers, and did not dare glance up.

"Why, you're trembling. Hey! You really are wet, and the wind has turned chilly." He bundled her shawl around her shoulders. "Come on!"

"I'm all right," she protested. "Are you going to stay long at Fort Kamloops?"

"Not if I let Mama's daughter catch cold. I'm afraid I didn't notice."

You didn't notice a whole lot of things, she thought as he hustled her homeward. But there would be tomorrow. Maybe many tomorrows!

"What's all the excitement?" he suddenly asked her.

She followed his gaze to the south bank. People were gathered around someone. They were pointing towards the old Okanagan Fur Brigade Trail. "I wonder what's happened! Only one way to find out." She darted for the canoe landing.

"Papa! What's the matter?" she asked, making straight for her father when they had reached the south bank.

"Och! Just some tenderfoot travelers who think they've been raided."

"Raided?" She grabbed his shirtsleeve.

But her father had eyes only for Connell. "You're a sight for sore eyes!" he said, shaking the young man's hand and thumping his shoulder. "And sure, Mama will be smothering you with fresh bread and butter."

"But Papa! What about the travelers?"

"They think they've been raided."

"Don't they know if they've been raided?"

"Och, they're tenderfeet, Meg. And tenderfeet scare fast. Myself, I think the camels just stumbled on them."

"The camels!"

"Sure you know what a camel stench does to a pack train," he said, reasonably.

She hid her exasperation under the pleasantness Mama demanded.

"You know how they are, Meg. Tenderfeet. These ginks think the Indians drove the camels on them on purpose."

"INDIANS!" She felt Connell's arm round her shoulders.

"You know how these miners are. Myself, I think the camels just happened to stumble on their camp."

Connell's arm was moving her towards the river.

"You're wet and you're going home. Right now. I'll paddle you over. Then I'll find out about the raid, Meg."

"But —"

"But nothing. You're going."

She went. Anyway, it would give her a chance to make herself pretty before he came in for supper. But a raid! The old chill caught her stomach. Indians using the camels to scatter a pack train!

Connell didn't say much about it when he came in; and he didn't seem to notice that she'd changed her dress and tied on a blue ribbon. He just kept them merry at the table with tales of his winter's adventures. He slipped out to the compound the moment he'd finished.

As soon as the dishes were washed, Megan followed. An air of excitement was stirring Fort Kamloops.

Connell strode straight towards her. "I'll be leaving tomorrow," he said, catching her hand up. "These miners want an outrider, and I was bound for the diggings anyway."

He was leaving. So soon! "It . . . it was a raid, Connell?"

"Perhaps. Perhaps not. In any case, you're safe in Fort Kamloops."

"Was it Indians?"

"Stay safe in Fort Kamloops, just in case!" he ordered Megan; and he laid his cheek on her hair for one wonderful moment. Then he pulled her along to say good-bye to the family. "They're camped along the trail there," he told them. "I'll see you as we go through tomorrow."

And he was gone.

Later, she took off the ribbon that he hadn't even noticed. He had not even seen her, much less the ribbon. If only she had known he would be here so briefly! If only she hadn't been so silly and gabby! If only she had dared to lift her hand tonight and lay it — once! — on his lean cheek. She flung herself on her bed.

A howl split the silence that lay on the big, lonely country. Other howls answered it out there in the starlight. Coyotes? . . . or . . . Indians?

She found herself shivering. "Here, the Indians are friendly," she told herself fiercely. "But yet it might have been a raid."

She kept tossing for hours. The friendly Shuswaps would *not* rise as the hostile Sioux had risen! . . . Or . . . would they?

7

"MAMA," MEGAN SAID FIRMLY AT SIX O'CLOCK THE NEXT morning, "he may be going through early and the least we can do is be out there."

"That's the least we can do," her mother agreed. "But the least is not enough to be doing for Connell. There's going to be a pound cake for that boy to take with him, and a batch of King Williams. So roll up your sleeves, Meg!"

"Yes, Mama. But what if we miss him?"

"With Willie out watching?"

By nine the cakes were oozing butter into the white cloth that wrapped them, as they lay inside an Indian basket. The house smelled of nutmeg and rose water. And when Willie burst in with the word that the pack train was coming, Megan whipped off her apron, dusted flour from her gray dress, perked up her yellow ribbon, and rushed to the south bank.

Connell was coming!

So were mules and packhorses.

He swung down from his strawberry roan only long enough to hoist Willie up into the air, shake Mr. Scully's hand vigorously, and give Mrs. Scully a hug while Megan hung the basket of cakes on his saddle horn. Then he snatched up her hands. "Many happy returns of the day, Meg!" He looked expectantly at her and seemed about to say more. Instead, he dropped her hands and sprang back into the saddle.

He was gone with a smile and a wave of his stetson. Gone!

"He's gone." Megan's shoulders sagged. Oh! Why had she acted like a lump of bread dough? "I could shoot myself!" she muttered, blinking back tears.

"Och, he'll be back," her father predicted. "He'll be back for more of Mama's King Williams."

"*Mama's* King Williams!" She kicked a stone.

"Meg!" her mother warned her.

"I'm sorry, Mama." She shook off a few teardrops and waved after the pack train just in case he should glance back.

"If it's any comfort to you, I told him you made them."

"Oh, Mama! Thank you."

"I'm not blind altogether."

"Are you blind, a teeny bit?" Willie asked her.

"Only when I need to be."

It occurred to Megan that her mother was like rasp-

102

berry vinegar — tart, but refreshing, and wonderfully sweet in spite of the tartness.

"'Tis your birthday," she was saying. "So you're free to go gallivanting for the rest of the day. Sixteen! Och, it's hard to believe you're sixteen."

"It is hard to believe I'm sixteen," Megan agreed, although not aloud. Why, oh why, couldn't she act like a woman?

With Connell gone, even a free day, a birthday, lost its shine. But Megan made the most of it, though she didn't get out the gold pan again.

Bright days followed each other, and soon even Megan had stopped worrying about the other incidents that happened the day Connell came and went so quickly. Then three frightened men staggered into the Fort from the old Fur Brigade Trail. Their horses had been cut loose and then scattered by camels. And after the raid, the travelers had discovered the raider's sign —a large flake of ponderosa pine bark trimmed around the edges and marked with vermilion to make a camel. Through the eye of the camel was knotted a thin thong, a thong that had tufts of red-painted feathers along it and was weighted at the end by a bullet.

"Indians!" Megan had a horrible sinking in her stomach.

Her mother put the backs of her hands on her hips. "Why in the name of creation did they turn those camels loose to give the Indians notions of using them for mischief?"

"What could the owner do with them, Mama?"

"It's what could the Indians do with them that bothers me, Meg."

"Och, Katie. This is the work of some crank. Sure we've no reason to think the Shuswaps are unfriendly," Papa said soothingly.

"Except the reason we're providing. White men rushing in to grab gold. Do you think these Shuswaps haven't heard of the Indian warfare in the territories these men come from?" She sagged in a long sigh. "And there's Connell out there in the wilderness with horses and obstinate mules on a muddy trail. It's like one of my own children was out there."

"Is it a horse or an obstinate mule that's like one of your children?" he asked her, winking at Megan. But his banter fell flat. "There's no raiding north of the Thompson River," he reminded her comfortingly. "The Cariboo Trail's quiet."

There was another raid south of the river. Another bullet trailing feathers and a ponderosa pine bark camel.

"Papa," Meg demanded that evening. "Are the Shuswaps rising? Like the Sioux did?"

Her father considered his answer while he lit his pipe from a sliver of wood he had poked into the fire. He took a few thoughtful puffs. "Meg, do you not think these camel signs seem a bit fancy for Indians?"

"You mean . . . ? Just some . . . bandit? A . . . a Robin Hood?" There was a book about Robin Hood in the Fort library.

"Aye, a back-handed Robin Hood. He doesn't even seem to take their money."

104

"A back-handed balderdash!" scoffed Mrs. Scully. "You two! And your stories! And your imaginations! Well! I've enough imagination myself to give you a plain order, young lady. You stay close to the palisades from now on! No mooning along the river!"

"No, Mama." Don't worry! Megan's scalp prickled. The Shuswap could be like the Sioux.

There was yet another raid on the same trail. Mr. Scully reported it when he came in from his customary evening stroll on the south bank, where travelers often camped while they took on supplies. "The men got out of their tent just in time to see the tail end of a camel and the Indian who drove it, and . . ."

". . . and . . . a camel sign," Megan suggested.

"Aye, a camel sign."

"Did you get to see it this time?"

"I did not. The police constable had got it; they've had a man patrolling."

"Papa, there's something more, isn't there?"

"There is, Meg. Do you know who was raided this time? Our old friend, Mr. Fencil."

"Good! Maybe it'll make him think twice about trying something with an Indian."

"I thought we'd seen the last of that scamp," said Mrs. Scully.

"Maybe we have." Megan felt she had a right to hope for something. "After this scare, maybe he'll head for a civilized place like San Francisco."

"Not a chance, Meg. That gink can't wait to get to a creek to try out his gold diviner."

"Gold diviner." Megan sat up alertly.

"Diviner . . . dowser. You've heard of a water-witch that swings down to show where there's underground water for a well. Mr. Fencil has a gold-witch. Mistletoe, he tells me, instead of hazel. And he swears it'll find gold."

She leaned eagerly forward. "Do you think it could, Papa?" If there was only some sure way of locating gold, perhaps Mama would be willing to move on. "Do you think it'll find the Mother Lode or something?"

It was her mother who answered. "With Mr. Fencil handling it, it'll find something for sure — trouble."

"Och, Katie! Men change."

"Well, I'll not hold my breath till he does. It's not healthy to have the likes of him near rebellious natives."

Megan looked at her anxiously, but she said no more. Instead she changed the subject abruptly. "Have we run out of tea, Meg?"

"I'll make it." Megan jumped up, thankful to do something. Thinking always came back to the threat from the Indians.

"We've a bit of cake left," her mother announced, moving to get it. "And a bit of spirit too, I hope. We've had both things before, Mr. Fencil and hostile Indians, and lived through it. So let's not be making a poor mouth about the one or the other." She shrugged cheerfully as she unwrapped the pound cake. "Anyway, we've all got to die sooner or later and we may as well face it."

"Now your cake's not that bad, Katie."

Megan laughed with the rest, but later, in bed, the old

fears came crowding back. Mr. Fencil was likely to regard that camel raid as an act of war by the Indians. His
men, he still had two of them, Papa said, were likely to
retaliate on the first Indian they encountered. Here the
law didn't allow you to shoot Indians. But what did Mr.
Fencil care about the rules? Maybe she ought to go over
to the south bank and sort of remind him that now he
was in a Colony where there was strict English law and
a Police Force and a hanging judge. While she was telling
him, she could see the gold diviner!

Next day she went over to the south bank on the pretext of taking fresh buttermilk to her father.

"Papa," she said, handing it to him, "it would be a
very good idea for somebody to remind Mr. Fencil that
this is a Crown Colony with strict laws and policemen
and a hanging judge and . . ."

". . . and a girl who's wild to see a gold diviner." His
blue eyes twinkled at her.

"Well, but Papa, he does need to be scared."

"I doubt you could scare the likes of him. Still, I've
no objection to your getting a squint at the gold diviner.
Be back here in ten minutes!"

"Yes, Papa."

She made her way past tents, campfires, and horses.
Men swept off their hats in a mannerly greeting; and
Megan smiled at them, sensing their loneliness away from
their families.

Then she saw him. She had forgotten how long and
lank Mr. Fencil was.

"Well! If it isn't Miss Wagon Train, Megan Scully!"

"Uh . . . Hello, Mr. Fencil."

Thank goodness he didn't offer his hand; it was busy shaking a small brass box. Something inside the box, dried seeds? tiny shot? snuff? golddust?, moved back and forth, startling the girl like a rattlesnake's warning. He had not changed one bit. He did need to be jolted out of his contempt for rules.

"I hear you've given up gold-seeking," he said, "and settled down as Hudson's Bay servants."

The word servants stung her. "Not settled," she protested. "It's just that it takes a big grubstake to go to the diggings. But we'll get there." She wished he would hold that box still. "I . . . I hear you have a gold diviner, Mr. Fencil."

"If it weren't packed away, I'd show it to you, Megan." He indicated several horses being packed by his men. "Ugly customers," Mama always called the men.

Megan grabbed at her scattered wits. This time she was not going to act like a lump of dough and then kick herself after. She was sixteen. She was going to act like sixteen. She scrambled around in her mind for some way to start the scaring. And her eyes lighted on a WANTED sign, tacked up on a pine tree.

"Uh . . . about our grubstake, Mr. Fencil. Maybe it won't take as long as you think. Maybe we'll be lucky and pick up a reward." She indicated the poster.

"Here?" He shiggled the box softly. "You don't think big gunmen would bypass a little hole-in-the-wall like Kamloops?"

Exactly the opening she needed!

"I'm sure they'd like to. But that's the thing about the Cariboo, isn't it? There are only two ways to get in or out . . . down the narrow Fraser Canyon or else through Kamloops. If you go off those trails you just . . . perish from mountains or timber or rattlesnakes or Indians or something. So even big gunmen have to go this way if they're afraid of being bottled up in the canyon." She felt she had brought that off rather neatly.

"Then your chances are good for informing and getting a grubstake." He was not one bit worried.

Oh, well! She had more facts to fire at him. And she got on with the firing. "Uh . . . I guess we can't count on a reward, though," she said with what she hoped was an unhappy look. "There aren't any gunmen around, are there? I mean . . . I guess they hear about Judge Begbie and his Hanging Tree and stay south of the border. I guess they hear about him being called *Law in the Saddle*. You've heard how he rides circuit, I suppose?"

"I've heard how he rides circuit. With a flowing black cape and theatrical nonsense. Wearing a ridiculous wig to hold court on a stump. He must look funny."

"Not to the gunmen," she flashed back. Too quickly. She made herself smile. She must not betray her purpose. "Isn't it strange to be in a Crown Colony?" she asked as conversationally as she could. "But the miners seem to like the *Queen's Peace* better than frontier justice and Indian trouble. They certainly back up the policemen. Oh . . . They have a Police Force here."

"Fifteen constables scattered over a wilderness bigger than Texas. They could use wings, poor fellows."

"Yes, but I guess the miners know the policemen have the redcoats to support them — you know, the Royal Engineers that the Queen sent out."

"One company. Too bad they're fully occupied rushing the Wagon Road through to the diggings."

"But there's the Queen's Navy, too," she suggested, rather lamely.

"I can't see how the miners get much comfort from the Queen's Navy." He smiled at her. "It's stationed over on Vancouver Island. But don't look so downcast, dear. Can't you see how all this helps you?"

"Helps me?" She swallowed.

"Yes, you, dear. The situation is not too forbidding after all to the big gunmen. You watch the trails. You'll get your reward for a grubstake if you keep your eyes open. Good luck, Megan!"

She dared not look at him. She felt her face reddening.

"Thank you for coming to see me, dear. You have cheered me up greatly. Are the camel raids making you nervous, Megan?"

"No. I mean, yes, naturally."

"Then it's my turn to cheer you up. You have nothing to fear from the Indians as long as your father is a Company servant. The Company post was the only thing spared when the Sioux swept through Georgetown. Remember?"

"There's a good reason why Indians don't attack the Company."

"I thought you would see that. Who else supplies

them with muskets for raiding?"

"But it sells the muskets for hunting, Mr. Fencil." The accusation surprised her.

"You're loyal, Megan, as a good servant should be. Now don't think I blame your Company. Not a bit! They're business men; and business is business even when it gets bloody."

She opened her mouth to protest. But words of her father's leaped into her mind, *Meg, don't you think these camel signs seem a bit fancy for Indians?*

Mr. Fencil saw his advantage and pressed it. "You can't blame a Company that's threatened with ruin by an invasion of settlers after two hundred years of absolute monopoly. What does any man do when his living is threatened?"

She finally spoke up, and her voice was indignant. "Mr. Fencil, the Company traders simply would not —"

"— would not what? What a strange way your mind works, child. I didn't accuse your nice masters of inciting rebellion, even though they are squawmen and even though they have sound commercial reasons for keeping the land Indian."

"I have to go, Mr. Fencil."

"Of course. You have to think things over. But do remember, dear. You have nothing in the world to fear from Indians as long as your father is a Company servant."

"I really must go."

She heard the tiny box shaking as she scudded away. She felt her heart pounding.

"Well!" her father greeted her. "And how did the scaring go?"

"It went backwards. Oh, Papa!" She grabbed his shirtsleeve.

"Then maybe you've found out that a snake should be avoided," he remarked comfortingly.

"About those camel raids, Papa . . ."

"About those camel raids, Meg." He lifted her chin with a work-roughened finger. "There are big things at stake in this colony. There are men who feel strongly, both white men and red men. I'm telling you this so you'll watch your step, darling, and not go poking your nose in where it wouldn't be wanted. This is a wilderness country, with little protection."

"So little protection!" A shudder ran through her.

"There's protection enough, mind. And you're a smart girl, Megan Scully."

"Not as smart as I thought I was ten minutes ago, Papa." She smiled ruefully at him. "You won't say anything to Mama?"

"I won't. And I don't think you will either." He winked and went back to the shelves he was building in the new store.

Megan went back to thinking about Indians and the Company. *There are big things at stake in this colony. There are men who feel strongly, both white men and red men.* Did Papa mean the Company?

But there were no more raids that week. And there were no reports of Indian trouble in the almost up-to-date copies of *The British Columbian:*

NEWS FROM CARIBOO . . . positively affirmed that $16,000 was taken out of the Hard Curry Claim in one day.

"Sixteen thousand in one day!" Megan gasped when she read it. In one day you could get rich and have a beautiful home and dresses. "Sixteen thousand in one day." She sighed.

Not as deeply as her mother sighed, however, when she read the paper. "Homesteads going for a dollar an acre. Farms springing up all along the trails to the diggings. Land speculators moving in!" She put her hands on her hips.

Megan frowned. Mama was a born settler. With the Company shorthanded from desertions, Mama was working in the dairy for a dollar a day. "That's an acre a day," she often reminded her family. "Or a few inches of a cow's leg."

"We'd get more money at Williams Creek even if we didn't go mining," her daughter pointed out. "Papa could get eight or ten dollars a day carpentering at the diggings." Here he got four dollars. "He'd get big pay there."

"And wouldn't he need to?" her mother answered, unimpressed. *"Flour raised to $1.25."*

Megan sometimes regretted that her mother could read.

They'd never get to the diggings.

8

EARLY MAY WAS NOISY AT THE FORT. FUR PRESSES
screeched. Horses whinnied. Whipsaws rasped, and ham-
mers banged on the south bank.

One day when her parents had gone back to work
and she had finished the noon dishes, Megan took Willie
across the river to see how the new trading post was
progressing.

For a moment the millions of tiny sunflowers on the
hills caught her fancy. It was as though the land, too,
was bursting with spring fever and gold fever. Then hearing a shout behind her, she glanced back at the river.

Mr. Stewart had summoned his paddlers. He, too, was
coming over. And as always he was splendid in broadcloth and beaver.

Willie didn't have to be admonished to stay back and
keep quiet. He practically held his breath. He lived in

115

awe of the Chief Trader.

"He's going to talk to Papa," he proudly predicted. Then he clung to his sister's hand, watching Majesty approach.

"We'll skin up to our lookout." Megan pulled him away to take him along a path that ran up one of the hills behind the new post. "Now watch out for rattlers!"

Reaching the special place she liked, she looked wistfully west. The trail lay like a buckskin thong along the base of green-and-gold hills and then turned north. The trail to the pot of gold. Restlessness raced through her. "I wish I were a boy, Willie!" A boy went where he wanted to. But not a girl! A girl's family enclosed her like palisades, keeping her stifled.

A vagrant breeze rolled a tumbleweed past her. It was an airy skeleton left behind by the early spring windstorms. She noticed its tentative advances, its hesitations. At the will of the wind! A girl was like that. She kicked a clump of bunchgrass.

Willie tugged her dress. "Look! Look!" His pudgy forefinger pointed along the trail that came in from the southwest, from the lower Fraser. A rider was flailing his horse towards Kamloops.

"K'lahma!" K'lahma, who seemed to be Mr. Stewart's personal messenger, was something of a dandy among the proud braves employed at Kamloops. Yet now mud spattered his fringed leggings and beaded tunic. His piebald was lathered.

Maybe there had been another camel raid. "Let's go down and see Papa," Megan urged Willie.

116

But Papa was still with Mr. Stewart as the Chief Trader inspected the building. And he stood deferentially away when K'lahma dismounted.

Whatever it was, the message angered Mr. Stewart.

"I guess K'lahma runned that good horsie too fast," Willie suggested. "I guess Mr. Stewart is mad at K'lahma."

"He's sure mad at somebody."

The old panic gripped Megan. And she watched apprehensively as the Chief Trader turned suddenly and strode towards his canoe, barking out an order.

His paddlers jumped to attend him. What on earth had happened?

She made straight for her father. "Papa, what's happened?"

"Not a thing."

"Not a thing?" Megan grabbed his shirtsleeve.

He glanced at her. "You're as white as a sheet. Och, I suppose you're busy again whipping up a scalping."

"Papa, please! What has happened?"

"Well, now . . ." He pondered whether to betray his eavesdropping. "I suppose you might call it rebellion."

"Rebellion!" She knew it. "The Shuswaps?"

"You might call it rebellion," he repeated mildly. "Involving a lady."

"A lady?"

"By the name of Miss Alison Stewart."

"Are the Indians after her?"

"If they are, they'll soon have good company, I'm thinking. Mr. Stewart himself will be off on that young lady's trail, if I'm good at predicting."

"Papa! How can you joke? Mr. Stewart was purple with rage."

"Now, Meg! He was only a fine gentle scarlet. I'll tell you this much, though it's none of our business, the girl's run off from school and is headed up this way. Her father'll change her direction, if I know Mr. Stewart. And a lucky thing, too. A fine state we'd be in here, with two strong-minded girls running life at Fort Kamloops."

"Papa!" She was suddenly jubilant. It wasn't Indian trouble! Instead, it was something wonderful. Another white girl at Fort Kamloops! "Oh, that'll be glorious, Papa! Wonderful! Wonderful!"

"It'll be wonderful for sure if she can ride down her father's objections. They like obedience in the Company."

"Yes." But there was more to this than disobedience. "Papa, do you think — ?"

"I think it's not for the likes of us to go poking our noses into their family matters."

"Of course not," Megan agreed. But one couldn't help wondering.

Her gaze swung westward. Any minute now a Colonial young lady might come cantering along in an elegant riding habit. Hunting-green velvet, perhaps, with a small beaver hat held securely by veiling . . . and a white silk cravat at her throat.

"Megan. Megan!" her father was saying. "Didn't I hear Mama say something about getting the potatoes into the stew early enough this time?"

Megan's vision vanished. In this family, you always bumped back to potatoes. She scowled.

118

"Meg wishes she was a boy, Papa."

"Does she now? Och, well. It takes a wise woman to know her own value."

"Oh, I know my own value. Unfortunately! And my own future. I'm doomed to get potatoes for ever and ever."

"You're doomed for worse things than that if Mama catches you pouting." He spanked her gayly along on her way to the canoe.

Megan frowned. Then she smiled. At least it was not Indian trouble that K'lahma had reported.

She put Willie out to watch while she worked at the stew. And he faithfully reported Mr. Stewart's departure, as Papa had predicted. Half an hour later he reported an arrival, though not that of Miss Stewart.

"Ross is here! Ross is here!" he cried out as he rushed in to tell Megan.

"Who is Ross?"

"Will you tell me?" he wistfully suggested.

Megan put her hands on her hips, discovering why Mama did it. "Tell me more, Willie!"

"Well, Johnny says it's Ross." Johnny was his favorite halfbreed playmate. "To see Alison."

That name touched her like a spur. She whisked off her apron, checked the fire, dumped the potatoes into the stew, and rushed out. Just in time to see the mysterious stranger disappearing into the Fort's store.

"Willie, I have to go to the store, too. We've run out of tea. But you stay right here by the house and keep your eyes open for a young lady. Don't you dare move."

"Not even if a bear comes?"

"Not even if a bear comes. Don't move for anything except a fancy young lady, a *white* lady."

Because of the forthcoming move to the south bank, and fortunately for Megan's purposes, the Company store was a shambles of boxes and barrels and piled blankets. Desertions to the goldrush had made Mr. Sutherland the lone storekeeper.

Her moccasins made no sound as she sneaked in and darted behind a red woolen mountain.

Ross was as tall as Connell; he towered above Mr. Sutherland as he faced him across a counter. Instead of a western hat, though, he wore a jaunty Scotch tam with a tall white eagle feather. Her mind flashed to the hero of *The Lady of the Lake*. But this boy was dark. His profile was lean and angry and his voice seemed angry, too. She caught his last sentence. "Those raids were reckless, futile things."

Was he accusing the trader?

Certainly Mr. Sutherland's voice was apologetic when he finally answered. "No one here ever intended to hurt you, laddie."

Hurt you! He, too, had been raided? But surely not on Company orders!

"Tell me what you need from the stores, laddie, and be on your way."

"Why?" Ross lifted his head, squared his shoulders under his fringed buckskin. "Why am I not welcome at the Fort? Why shouldn't I wait to see Alison?"

"Alison? How is it you know that she's coming? Did

you have something to do with her foolish defiance?"

"Is defiance always foolish?" Ross' voice had hardened.

As Megan strained to hear the trader's answer, she realized that eavesdropping was undignified. Yet wild horses could not have dragged her away. Not even Mama!

"Aye, defiance is foolish. There are always better ways to achieve what you're wanting." Mr. Sutherland's voice was troubled, and he sighed as he turned to busy himself with tradesgoods.

"I'll need more shot than that, and more powder, sir." Ross spoke crisply, asserting his customer-privilege, yet retaining a respect for the other's position.

The trader sighed again. "'Tis a poor way to live. Especially for a MacNeil."

"There are poorer ways," the young man retorted. Were his words tinged with a dark accusation?

Were the traders doing something underhanded to stem the white invasion that was ruining their business?

"The Company could use a good man with the horses." Mr. Sutherland was coaxing. A bribe for the boy's silence?

"I've other plans for my time, sir."

"Aye, but are they good plans?"

The answer was whipped out like a dagger. "By whose code should I judge?" He thudded down a gold-poke. "Give me twice as much shot and powder as last time, if you please, Mr. Sutherland."

"Aye." Mr. Sutherland turned away to comply.

Ross silently fingered a fan made of red plumes. "Red

Feather," he muttered, and slipped it through his waist-band. "I'll take this."

The trader merely nodded. He weighed out the cost in golddust while Ross stowed things in buckskin saddle-bags. "Away with you, now, laddie," he urged. "Come back when it blows over."

Ross stiffened. He stood as bristlingly straight as a spruce tree. "I'll go," he agreed. "But I'll be back soon. And I'll remind you, sir, that things don't always blow over." And as if he had had a sudden thought, he pulled off his bonnet and wrenched out the white feather.

Megan gasped. A white feather was a peace sign.

He plucked a small red plume from the fan in his waistband and put it into the silver crest. And not until he had carefully replaced his now-red-feathered bonnet did he swoop up his bags and stride out of the building.

Had he declared war on the Company? Megan held her breath. She saw something drop as he swept through the doorway. But she waited until the trader had moved to enter his sales in the Company ledger. Then she darted out like a swallow and skimmed up the dropped thing as she flew from the building.

Dislodged from his sash, likely, it was a flake of pon-derosa pine bark, trimmed and painted to resemble a stylized camel. It had a hole for an eye.

Megan swallowed. She dropped it into her pocket as if it were slimy. So he *had* been raided. Maybe, before she came in, he had waved the camel sign angrily under the trader's nose.

It was horrible to think of!

By the time she got to the palisade gate, his furious stride had carried him to the river. Two lounging paddlers sprang towards a dugout.

MacNeil! Of course. There had been a Chief Trader MacNeil. Naturally the Fort treated his son with respect. And naturally the Company wouldn't want him hurt if . . . if . . .

But she just couldn't believe that nice men like Mr. Sutherland could have anything to do with the terrifying camel raids. Yet why was the Company post the only thing in Georgetown not burned by Sioux raiders?

On the south bank, as the canoe arrived, a horse was led out of the shade of a cottonwood. A mettlesome black with a glinting browband. Ross mounted and cantered away, eastward.

Well! Several things besides springtime were stirring at Kamloops. And one of them seemed to be a defiant love affair. Megan longed to help the swashbuckling young man and his golden-haired lady. He was obviously a halfbreed, and so, no doubt, unacceptable to Mr. Stewart. Lines from *Young Lochinvar* leapt into her mind:

"I long wooed your daughter. My suit you denied.
Love swells like the Solway and ebbs like its tide.
And now I am come with this lost love of mine . . ."

That's who he was like, Young Lochinvar. And she aimed to help him. Dropping her hand into her pocket, Megan gave a startled squeal. *The camel sign!* How could she ever explain it to Mama?

But then should she show it to Mama at all? It would only bring on sharp questions, specific orders, strict prohibitions.

She had not quite decided by evening when she settled by the candle with her book and her daydreams. She began to think of star-crossed lovers.

"Mama," she said dreamily by and by, "in Mr. Shakespeare's *Romeo and Juliet,* Juliet was fourteen. Two years younger than I am!"

"Is that a fact?" Mama was unimpressed.

"Yes, it is a fact." Lacking a more sympathetic confidante, Megan went on. "Think of it, Mama! A romantic heroine dying for love at fourteen! Well?" she demanded. "Mama! Don't you think . . . something . . . about it?"

"I do. I think if she'd been older, that girl, she'd have had more good sense and lived longer."

"Mama!" Megan was shocked. Then she sighed in resignation. That was what you expected of Mama. She climbed back into her newest daydream, using her book as a screen to keep out intruders. This daydream had Connell ambushed by the Shuswap on his way back to Kamloops, left lying, injured . . . while she came up, impelled by a strange hunch. She flung herself off her horse, lifted his dear head to her bosom —

Bosom? She glanced scathingly down at herself. Juliet must have been more developed at fourteen. Catching her mother's sharp eye, she felt herself blushing. *Could* people read your thoughts?

"Are you not feeling well, Meg? You do look a bit flushed."

"Oh, Mama!" she protested.

"And you're quiet this evening."

"I'm enjoying my book."

"Are you now? Then you'll enjoy it all the more if it's turned around this way." She switched the book right way up, then began patching Willie's torn pants.

Megan tried to recapture her daydream. Now where had she come to? Oh yes. Connell's head was . . . no. She would just skip that part. And she frowned, concentrating.

"You haven't a cramp in your stomach?"

"Oh, Mama! Of course not."

"Hm." Mrs. Scully rose from her chair and went straight to the cupboard. She picked up a spoon and a jar of dark stuff. "Now open your mouth, Meg!" she ordered. "This is nothing but brimstone and treacle. Spring tonic."

"But—" Sulphur and molasses were gritty and awful!

"Well, if you'll not take it like a lady, you'll take it like a child." She grabbed the girl's nose by a thumb and forefinger; and when Megan opened her mouth to breathe, her mother plunged the spoon in.

She spluttered and protested. "I was feeling fine, Mama."

"You'll feel better still tomorrow."

Megan felt rebellion rising. How on earth could you ever feel grown-up around someone like Mama? No wonder girls defied their parents! And that settled it. She would not tell Mama about the camel sign. She was not going to answer ten hundred thousand questions and be humiliated. She would hide it at the bottom of her Indian basket, under the ribbons and the Williams Creek nugget. She had stood up to do just that when her father sprinted in.

Alert to his moods, she knew this was one of those times when his gold fever was rising.

"Well, Kate," he began, "there'll be little enough grass growing this year on the trails to the goldfields. The word's got around of the strikes they were making last fall when snow cut off the mining."

There had been Cameron's strike: pay dirt forty feet thick, and rich all the way down to bed rock. Billy Barker had struck dirt that washed out at five dollars a pan. Diller had taken out a hundred and two pounds of gold in one day. "And that's worth twenty thousand good American dollars. Och, it's staggering! The gold that's just lying there waiting!"

"Papa!" Megan said. "Why, we might go to the creeks for not even a month and come back with enough gold to . . . to . . ." Her mind bogged at the thought of the Scully fortune.

"Indeed we might do that," her mother agreed. "And then again we might go in for the whole blessed summer and come out with just holes in our pockets and no roof over our heads for the winter that's coming. We've a family to think about, Robert Hugh Scully."

"We've a family to think about." He picked up her words like a stone to polish. "And no farm of our own yet, nor the money to stock it. Perhaps when the gold is so thick it's a family that should take its chances. Och,

Katie!" He turned coaxing. "I know it's the children you're thinking of. And after yon trek through the Rockies, who's to blame you for fearing this venture? But it's different ahead. There's stopping places galore. And there's food for the asking."

"So they tell me. But 'tis them that is doing the asking. For one pound of flour they're asking more than a dollar. And they're asking a whole dollar for a candle the size of a starving rat's tail. Not to mention the danger of a raid of camels."

"Camels! A wild notion some gink has picked up and then dropped like a hot potato. Have you heard any more of that business?" he challenged.

"I have not," she admitted. "But then I don't hear too much, getting on with my work instead of strolling round the campfires every evening." She waved Willie's pants at him.

"The camel raids are over."

Megan lowered her eyes and kept perfectly silent. They probably were over now that Ross had declared war.

"The Cariboo Trail is safe, Katie."

It probably was, too. There hadn't been one camel raid north of the Thompson.

"I'll tell you how safe, Kate. Last summer Diller took out seventy-five thousand dollars in golddust and nuggets by himself, with one friend. They went all the long way down that wilderness trail without one bit of trouble from red man or white man."

"That was last summer."

"I think I'll go to bed now." Megan felt vaguely uneasy, though not uneasy enough to divulge her secret.

At least she'd keep the sign hidden until Miss Alison's arrival. She might need an excuse to approach a Colonial young lady.

9

MEGAN WANTED TO BE OUT ON WATCH FOR THE CHIEF Trader's daughter; but Mrs. Scully had two days off from the dairy and meant to accomplish miracles.

So instead of dreaming romantic dreams, she swirled a scrub brush over the floorboards, seething with frustration. "You know, Mama," she finally burst out. "I feel sorry for those poor smelly camels."

"Do you now?" Her mother was making quick biscuits, standing on a rush mat that protected a scrubbed part.

"Mr. Sutherland says camels are highly regarded in their own country because of their humps and special eyelids and footpads. Here they have all that for nothing. They're tragically misplaced. Designed for one kind of a life and forced into another." She shot a glance at her mother before adding, "Like me," as if that little comparison had just occurred to her.

"And like this bottle," her mother agreed, holding up her rolling pin.

Foiled again, Megan watched her mother's hands cut rounds of dough with a tumbler that had also started life as a brandy bottle. It had been transformed into a glass by burning a cord around its middle, knocking off the top, and then filing the edges. The dough *whooshed* and clung to it, but was quickly tapped off. Mama no more stood for nonsense from dough than from a daughter.

"Designed for one kind of a life and forced into another, are you? Well, I've news for you, darling. Every woman is designed to give comfort and courage; and a dirty house helps neither one nor the other. Put that in your pipe and smoke it; and if you still feel you resemble a heathenish camel, just consider what happened to them when they weren't kept busy. The Devil finds work for idle hands. So get on with your work, young lady!"

"Yes, Mama."

It was evening before she escaped. Flame was streaking gray clouds above low hills. Scattered pines climbed the rise, crowding up near the top as if for a glimpse of the glory that seemed to wait over the skyline. They were like gold seekers, she thought; and those stragglers below — they were like the Scullys, unlikely to see it. She sighed, and glanced around at the olive-green bulk of the hills, at the heather-rose rim shading up into blueness. It all seemed so big and so empty and so terribly terribly quiet.

Coyotes started up their thin, chilling chorus.

Why didn't she hurry, the Chief Trader's daughter? What you needed here was something to keep your mind busy, not your hands. Something other than coyotes and Indians and a camel sign you had hidden.

By one o'clock the next day, her patience was like eggshell. "You're sure you haven't seen a white lady come in yet?" she demanded of Willie.

"I seed Lolo come," he parried. Lolo was an ancient, important chief. "And I seed a Indian lady come out, a young Indian lady. She went that way." He pointed eastward, along a path by the river.

Lolo's granddaughter, she guessed. One half the men in the Fort were in love with her. "Willie, you're to come in. Mama says!"

As soon as Megan had the dishes out of the way she resolutely faced her mother. "Mama, do you realize that I haven't had a chance to do any history lately, or figuring?"

"I do." Mrs. Scully glanced up from the bread she was kneading. "It's come very sudden, this interest in lessons. Still, I have worked you hard lately. So I will let you go gallivanting. You'll need to go down to the river where it's quiet to study?"

Megan flushed. "Mama, sometimes I think you're a very smart woman."

"Do you now? Then you'd better skedaddle before I start figuring out what bee is buzzing round in your bonnet this time."

"Yes, Mama. I'm going." She grabbed books and a shawl and dashed out.

The compound seemed drowsy, though there were thuds in the fur loft. In the shade of a bastion, an Indian wife stitched moccasins while her papooses crooned to wooden dolls.

Megan made straight for the canoe landing to scan the trails. Not a sign in the West of the Chief Trader's daughter. And no messenger booting his horse in from the East. The raids had stopped. Maybe that's what Lolo the old Head Chief had come to talk about. If the Company was involved. And his granddaughter? Megan couldn't help wondering *which* man she was meeting.

Concerned mainly with how best to disguise her real motives, she glanced at her books in triumph. A scholarly look could hide snooping superbly. By lucky chance, she had picked up *The Indian Trade Language of the Pacific Coast*. Not an actual language, this Chinook Trade Jargon mixed Indian, English, and French words. She strolled along slowly, trying out the Jargon. *Canim:* a canoe. *Kla-how-ya:* the friendly salutation. *Skookum:* strong. *Skookum tumtum:* strong heart, brave. Her feigned scholarliness grew real as she made her way along the river: walking, pausing, walking, practicing words she'd be sure to need on her way to the diggings.

As she rounded a clump of willows, a girl sprang square in her pathway, a girl in a doeskin shift and a beaded headband.

"Uh . . ." The book gave no advice as to what to say to Lolo's granddaughter. "Uh . . . *Kla-how-ya,*" Megan ventured. But the friendly salutation seemed to fall flat between them.

133

Then she saw Ross bristling straight as a spruce in the shade of the willows.

"Oh, I'm . . ." She was flabbergasted.

"Did the Company send you to find me?" The native girl's flawless English was only one more surprise.

"No." Megan felt foolish. Why oh why hadn't she just said a casual Hello?

"You must be Megan Scully." The voice was full of contempt and the gaze seemed to take in all the mussiness of her gray dress and the stains on her moccasins. "Megan Scully, snooping the way white girls do."

"Snooping?" The truth pricked like a cactus needle. "I'm simply looking for a quiet place to study." She flourished her books.

But the Indian girl was no longer listening to Megan.

"K'lahma's coming," she said; though Megan could hear
nothing. "Ross!" Her tone was pleading. Her hand mo-
tioned him away.

He stood straighter. "Let him come, Alison."

"Alison!" Megan's mouth dropped open. Like everyone else here, Alison Stewart had an Indian mother and
not the golden-haired lady in the portrait. This was Alison
Stewart meeting Ross. No wonder she was angry at
Megan's intrusion. "Let me help you," she offered.

"We don't need you. Fortunately. I found out at
school that white girls are silly, vain, stupid, weak, spineless tattletales."

"Spineless?" Megan picked up just one of the insults.
She whirled around to face Ross. "You needn't be afraid
I'll betray you," she burst out on impulse. "I give you my

promise." She warmed to the glow that sprang up in his dark eyes. She liked Ross!

Now Megan heard the horse.

"Please go, Ross!" Alison entreated. "Or they'll pack me back to Victoria."

"No they won't," Megan announced. She grabbed the surprised girl's arm, yanked her around the willows, pushed her down onto the grass by the side of the trail, and said, "Teach me Chinook!" She'd show her who was spineless.

But as K'lahma reined up near them Alison rose haughtily, dusting bits of twig from her beautiful doeskin. A torrent of words fell from the tall Indian, but only once did the halfbreed girl move, and that was to cross her hands above the beaded embroidery of her dress, as though to defend her Indian apparel. She spoke once, in English. "Why should I wear ugly, uncomfortable dresses?"

"Your father is waiting to tell you why," he answered, also in English. And he wheeled his piebald to return to the stockade.

In disdainful silence, Alison watched him go. Then she whirled on Megan. "I've noticed before that white girls take readily to deception."

Without a word, Megan started for home, her shoulders square, her own rebellion aroused.

"Well, now!" her mother remarked as she entered the kitchen. "Who threw a rock at Meg Scully? Or was it only some word that was too close for comfort?"

Megan grabbed about for some suitable answer.

"Mama! Alison Stewart's a halfbreed."

"Is she now?" Mrs. Scully calmly accepted the start-ling disclosure. "And what did you expect in a land where white women are backward in coming? Have you had your eyes closed all winter? So she's a halfbreed."

"But Mama! She's the Chief Trader's daughter."

"And don't you be forgetting it!" her mother said sharply.

Megan was glad to escape to bed early that night. Why did Alison want to look like an Indian instead of a Colonial young lady? And since she wasn't a Colonial young lady after all, why did Mr. Stewart object to Ross as a suitor? She finally went to sleep, and without once thinking about whether or not the Shuswaps were rising.

In the morning, the questions were still with her. Why had Mr. Stewart banned Ross? What on earth had he done? Whatever it was, he was not ashamed of it. He had wanted to face K'lahma. She intended to find out a few answers. But she was not going to face that Alison again in work-stained clothes. She was not going to be undermined by a contemptuous glance at dried spots of gravy.

"Mama," she said firmly, "did you happen to notice how mussy all of my clothes are?"

"And did you happen to notice it's a fine day for washing? Or would you be like a misplaced camel at the wash tub out there by the back door?"

"I could take a chance on it since I'd like to look decent." She was deep in the suds when the shadow fell on her.

137

"Kla-how-ya."

Startled by the voice, she glanced up. K'lahma!

"You will ride with the Chief Trader's daughter. At once." He spoke and was gone, like the swoop of an eagle.

What a curt invitation! Or was it an order? "Mama!" she called, scraping off suds as she dashed through the doorway. She poured out the news. "But what on earth can I wear?" She glanced down in despair at her water-slopped brown dress. Her gray dress was in the wash. Her old buckskin pants from the trek were a tattered relic. She had a blanket dress; but it was too skinny to go over a saddle. "Oh, Mama!" she wailed. "What on earth can I wear?"

"There's only your new dress."

"The *squiggle* dress?" Aghast, the girl thought of its hideous pattern. "Could I wear your light-brown skirt, Mama?"

"You can if you don't mind looking like you'd poked your head up through the smokehole of some Shuswap's tepee."

"Maybe we could fix it."

"If we'd time. Which we haven't. At once, the man said; and it's not for the likes of us to keep the Stewarts waiting." She bustled into the bedroom to whisk out the new dress. "Och, it's not as bad as you think, Meg."

"It couldn't be." She couldn't bear to look at it. That dress was a tragedy or a joke, depending on whether you did or did not have to wear it.

"The green'll go fine with a bit of hair ribbon."

"And the worms will go fine with the way I feel."

138

"You'll feel none the better for standing there sagged like a dismal, wet cedar. It's your shoulders that count and not what you hang on them. Don't forget that a lady is known by her backbone, not her velvets."

Reluctantly Megan shed the wet brown dress.

"Now!" her mother warned. "No poor mouth about it! There's dignity, Meg, in making the best of whatever you have. So hold up your head, and put your sunbonnet on, or your nose will be peeling like a birch tree."

"Sunbonnet too?" Surely she could be spared that last degradation!

It descended like doom; her mother fastened the hooks. "The most important thing any girl wears is the look on her face. If you remember that, you'll do us proud. Och, the dress fits and it's neat and it's clean."

"And it's hideous." Megan blinked back her tears as she slipped out the door. She fled to the corral before courage could fail her. She seemed destined for humiliation.

One glance at her riding companion made her long to crawl under a stone with her squiggles around her.

Obviously Miss Alison was obeying her father's command to ride out with Fort Kamloops' one white girl. There was nothing of yesterday's Indian maiden about the horsewoman who mounted the fiery, big, golden-chestnut, nothing except a controlled, savage fury. Her blue bodice was faultlessly tailored as was her riding skirt of blue velvet. Her shining black hair flowed out from under a straight-brimmed Spanish hat, held by a thong. Alison Stewart's elegance seemed to glisten like the silver inlay decorating the butt that protruded from her carved-leather rifle-bucket. Even her carbine had obviously been specially designed for her, the first Lady of a small, frontier empire. She looked competent and courageous, and as belonging as the big airy ponderosas and the silver-gray sagebrush. "Good morning, Megan." It could have been the Chief Trader.

"Good morning, Miss Stewart." Megan climbed up on Klukuhl, a brown mare apparently chosen for an inexpert rider. Klukuhl was a small gloomy creature with large, shaggy fetlocks. Glumly deploring the bunch-up of her hideous skirts and the swing-down of her awful sun-bonnet, she leaned over to check her stirrup. "Ooooooo!" A dried splash of gravy showed on her moccasin. And her temper exploded.

She should have had more time to get ready. What did these lordly Stewarts think they were ordering people out on ten minutes' notice? This was a Colony now. People were free, not Company servants. Annoyance and mortification burst out in one angry comment.

"If you had given me time, Alison Stewart," she heard herself saying, "I could have been properly dressed instead of wearing stuff designed for savage Indian tastes. Oh!" She gasped in dismay. What had she said!

Alison's dark eyes flashed. "Made for the white man's conception of Indian tastes," she retorted. "Follow me!" The words were a curt command. Kalitan bounded towards the rolling rangeland.

Megan shook off her angry tears and dug in her heels. She had worsened things by her silly pride. No. It had not

140

been pride, she admitted. Real pride would have held her head high and her foolish mouth shut. It was shortage of pride that made you try to prove something that shouldn't need proving. The squiggle dress was a tragedy indeed when worn by a silly, vain, stupid, weak, spineless white girl. Then there was no more time to think, only time to try to keep up with the mad pace Alison Stewart set.

The Chief Trader's daughter finally reined in and waited beside a small lake. A muskrat moved off in a big V of ripples.

"You're like the rest of the gold-seekers, aren't you?" she said, as Megan rode up. She held her mount in, as if she intended to stop only briefly.

"In what way?" Megan asked, her voice soft and respectful.

"You scorn the natives."

"Oh no. I do not." All she scorned was herself.

"You think the Indians are savage."

"Oh no!" What on earth could she say to placate Alison? Yet, remembering the Sioux massacre, how could she say that they weren't savage, either? Her eyes shifted from her companion to the horse, Kalitan, who was pawing the bunchgrass. "Alison," she began, and her voice came out lamely, "the Indians where I lived, the Sioux Indians, massacred the white settlers."

"And why not?"

"Why not!"

"Yes, why not? When you whites wouldn't honor the treaty you made with them? Your government guaranteed payment for lands granted by the Sioux. And then, year

141

after year, it went back on its promise. You know just one side of the story. Well, I know the other. I know that last year a thousand Sioux waited six weeks for payment, away from their homes and their hunting. And what did they get for their patience? Contempt and starvation. Hungry families. Why shouldn't they massacre people who cheat them and rob them and scorn them?"

"But the settlers — "

"The settlers *here* haven't even a treaty; whites have no rights at all in the Colony, as you may soon find out."

Megan gasped. "You mean the British haven't a treaty with — "

"They don't think they need one. Savage? I'll tell you who's savage. Your own overlanders."

"Oh!" Megan gathered her breath in sheer indignation. Those travelers savage? She remembered their patience across the hot prairies, their dogged persistence in the awful spruce swamps, their final courage in tackling a wild unknown river in rafts.

"Has nobody told you about Mr. Rennie?"

"Mr. Rennie?" There had been three Mr. Rennies, three brothers. At Tête Jaune Cache, where the group had divided after crossing the Rockies, the Rennies had headed northwest, venturing out on the turbulent Fraser in roughly-made dugouts. "Did they drown?"

"Mr. Rennie was *eaten*."

"By wolves?"

"By his comrades. By the men he had rescued from the river." Alison flung the story at her like a blood-dripping scalplock. Mr. Rennie had been injured while rescuing friends from a rock in the river. And he had been left with the friends while his brothers trudged through the snow to Fort George for help. When they returned with Indian guides to carry him out, they found him partly eaten by the men he had rescued. "There was only one leg left and part of an — "

"Oh, don't!" Megan begged her. "I don't believe it. I do not believe it."

"Mr. Rennie was eaten by the white men he had rescued."

"Oh no! Not by white men!"

"See? Not by white men!" Alison snatched at her words. "As if white-skinned people could never be savage. That's the way you all think and feel."

"But I just don't believe it," moaned Megan.

"Then I suggest that you ask Mr. Sutherland; and that you look right into his eyes when you ask him."

"But — "

"But they're white men, you mean? Good, civilized white men? Like the traders who sell smallpox blankets to Indians?"

"Smallpox blankets?"

"You never hear of the horrible things white men do."

"Your father is a white man," Megan dared to remind her.

"Yes, a Hudson's Bay trader, not a greedy gold-grabber. My father came west at eighteen to spend his whole life here. He married a chief's daughter and respected her people. Why do you think the Indians stay at peace with the Company? Why do you think those Sioux left the Company alone when they massacred the settlers? Why do you think you overlanders were able to cross the plains without one attack on your weak little carts? Did you ever think WHY?"

Mr. Fencil's words flew into her mind: *Who else supplies muskets for raiding?* But she pushed the thought from her.

"You don't think. You just grab."

Megan's indignant glance swept the other girl's fine clothing, then her own hideous cotton. "I haven't grabbed much."

"You intend to."

"Yes, I do. And that's what's the matter with you, Miss Alison. You Company people don't want anyone else butting in on *your* grabbing. You hate us because we are spoiling the fur trade and your monopoly of a rich country. And besides," she went on, warming up to her subject, "your traders came here in the first place for money. Don't pretend different! And you don't like our traders because they're competition."

"Because they're death. They sell smallpox for money." Amazingly, Alison's eyes filled with tears. Her proud shoulders sagged as Kalitan's reins slipped through her fingers, and he lowered his head to the tender young bunchgrass.

Shocked, Megan saw a tear drop to the handsome saddle. Soft words came to her lips; but there was no chance to say them.

"You need to learn a few things, Miss Megan Scully." Alison brought up her mount's head. "Follow me!" Kali-

144

tan bounded forward.

What was she planning with such fury? Well, whatever it was, a white girl had better not flinch. Megan dug in her heels. Whatever it was she had better not prove herself a silly, vain, stupid, weak, spineless tattletale.

10

For the next hour it seemed as if one of the native evil spirits had entered the Chief Trader's daughter.

Something worked in her like a ferment. Following her, Megan thought of the astounding tear. What if some Indian relative had died because of an infected blanket? Did the Indian Blood Code demand a white's death for a native's? Megan pushed down her terror as she urged her mare on. She'd be *skookum tumtum* if it killed her.

Alison finally stopped by some jackpine near the edge of another small lake; and she held herself as straight as the rushes. "Get down," she ordered as she dismounted. "Are you all right?" Her words seemed a challenge.

"Yes, thank you, Miss Stewart."

"Good." She loosed Kalitan to graze.

Though Alison just stood gazing at the water, there was menace there still. Glancing over at her horse, she called his name sharply, darted to him, and jerked his head away from what looked like peavine.

"Don't you let him eat vetch?" Megan asked, not so much to make conversation as to prove that she could.

"Vetch? Don't you know locoweed when you see it? Do you have to wait until the staggers develop?" With a look of scorn Alison sprang into her saddle and spurred Kalitan.

Megan mounted again and followed warily. There was something about to happen. But the sun was high before Alison stopped again on a lakeshore.

"Are you hungry?"

"Well, I am used to eating at noon."

"Nicely cooked meat," Alison suggested. "Or bread or cake. White people can starve, or eat one another, while there is food all around them."

"Look! I've eaten my share of trail food. I've lived on berries. And skunks! White girls aren't necessarily helpless and silly and squeamish, you know."

"No doubt you have eaten rat-tail then."

"I know what it is." She did, too. It was a sort of wild carrot that smelled like a parsnip. Since fur traders used it in wilderness travel, it couldn't be too revolting. Still, she screwed up her face in distaste at the mud-dripping roots Alison swooped up from the edge of the water.

"Will you have this for dinner?"

"Not all muddy like that." Megan snatched the roots and swished them clean. She would not act squeamish. She would gulp them down quickly no matter how horrid. But the parsnippy smell made her wrinkle her nose as she raised them to eat them.

Alison knocked them aside. "Two inches of that would drop you stone dead."

Megan found herself trembling. "Do you have to kill me to prove that white people know less than Indians? That they would have to eat one another to stay alive in an emergency?"

Alison ignored the question. "Which way is the Fort?"

Which way *was* the Fort? She hadn't been concentrating on landmarks. In sudden panic, she glanced about. More by hunch than by judgment, she made her decision. "That way."

"Then ride that way. I'll follow."

Megan mounted. She even fixed her sunbonnet. No use adding sunstroke to her other troubles. Then a bright notion hit her. She'd give Klukuhl her head. Holding her reins very loosely, she dug in her heels and whispered, "Take me home, Klukuhl. Home!"

It was some time before she began to get really worried. If only she had been more observant! Who knew where she was heading? Or when Alison would dart off and leave her.

Ahead stretched a bit of flat rangeland, sparsely spotted with sagebrush. "Klukuhl, take me home!" she implored; and she scanned the hills around her as she spurred the mare.

Klukuhl plunged heavily ahead.

Kalitan bounded after.

Without warning, it happened. Alison yelled *"Shugo-*

poots!", and the mare jumped sideways and reared, throwing her rider off into the sagebrush. Then she bolted.

Caught in horror, Megan watched Kalitan rear a few horses' lengths from her. His legs lashed out in her stupefied direction. Had the locoweed crazed him? Or was *shugopoots* a signal?

"The Blood Code," she gasped without knowing she said it. Unable to move, she saw Alison bring down her mount's head and in one flashing movement draw her carbine and dismount. Her rifle came instantly up to her shoulder.

"Don't shoot!" Megan screamed.

The girl's rifle cracked. And Megan heard a *thump* on the ground close beside her. She leaped to her feet, then sank back in horror. There, just a few feet away, a rattlesnake writhed, its ugly head smashed. She tumbled back, shuddering against a sagebush. She covered her face with her hands, scarcely feeling the deft hands that searched her for injury. Then, before she could gather herself together at all, Alison dashed off to call back the frightened horses.

"Kalitan!"

The golden-chestnut stood hesitant up on a slope; while the terrified mare galloped off beyond recall.

Megan's eyes ventured back to the dead thing. But for Alison's action — Shuddering, she closed her eyes before blurting out, "You . . . you saved my life."

Alison did not glance around. Her attention was centered on Kalitan's hesitant movements. She seemed intent

149

on allaying his fright and suspicions, on coaxing him down from his refuge.

Tensed and snorting, he ventured towards her a little. Alert to the slightest new threat to his safety, he moved down the slope and on through the sage in stiff-legged response to his mistress's coaxing. When he neared her, she went out to meet him, her movements and words soothing. As she reached him, she patted his neck, speaking to him in Shuswap.

Suddenly, he threw up his head, startled.

Beyond him, sweeping over the rise, came a small group of horsemen. Indians!

Hand upraised, the tall leader reined in with a quiet "Kla-how-ya." He and Alison exchanged comments in Shuswap. The group listened intently to what Alison told them and to directions she appeared to be giving. Then, with a courteous nod to the horsemen, she mounted Kalitan and streaked off, leaving Megan alone with the Indians!

Panic gripped her.

"Come." The leader leaned towards her with dark hand extended; other hands hoisted her up behind him.

She grabbed at his sash when he kicked his horse forward. Where were they taking her? She would *not* scream! She would *not* faint! She would die *skookum tumtum.*

She didn't even notice her bleeding arm until she glimpsed the Fort. *You have nothing to fear from the Indians as long as your father is a Company servant.* Mr. Fencil had been right . . . about . . . how much?

Now, only now, Megan's mind began to work again. And she recalled with horror that in that moment of peril, when Alison had acted with instant competence, she herself had shown hysteria. "Don't shoot!" she had screamed, betraying the depth of her distrust of the Chief Trader's daughter. That scream had been the final proof of her feelings, no matter what she might claim to feel or even think she felt.

Cringing inwardly, she felt worse by the minute. What might Alison not do now? "You'll do us proud," Mama had predicted. Well, she had not done them proud. She had failed them. She glanced at the dress that had started the quarrel. Truly it was a tragedy when worn by a silly, vain, stupid, weak, spineless white girl. Only one good thing about it. It was ruined.

They took her to Mrs. Sutherland. She wished they had taken her home; she longed for her mother's brisk comfort. Yet she was thankful they had not taken her home; she dreaded the questions. And Mama was at the dairy.

Redheaded Jeannie Sutherland looked her over.

"I don't think I have any bones broken," Megan said, and she managed the ghost of a smile. "The rattlesnake didn't have time to —"

"Don't think about the snake," Mrs. Sutherland advised as she stirred a liquid.

It wasn't the snake, actually, that haunted her. It was people: dark furious people, white cannibal people.

"Mrs. Sutherland," she whispered, "is it true what she said about Mr. Rennie?"

Mrs. Sutherland's hands stilled for a moment. She looked down at Megan. "Why does a rattlesnake strike?" she asked. "Many ugly things spring from the instinct of self-preservation."

"You mean . . . they *did* . . . eat him."

"The Indians say, 'Never judge a man until you have walked a mile in his moccasins.' Keep your mind on the why, Megan. On what drove them to do it."

"But white men!" She could not help blurting it out.

"Are the same inside as red men. And they have less knowledge of how to survive in the wilderness. Come now. Drink this. It will make you feel better."

A parsniplike odor rose from the cup. Megan pushed it away with a shudder. "I've had a bad sort of day," she explained. "That smell made me think of something."

Mrs. Sutherland sipped the liquid serenely before again coaxing her patient.

Megan drank it, her thoughts still aswirl with questions. "Mrs. Sutherland, you told me to keep my mind on the why. Then why . . ." She hesitated, like a canoe poised at the edge of rapids. And then she plunged in with mixed panic and daring. "Why does Alison hate us white people? Why is Ross not welcome? Why is someone scaring off the miners with camel raids?" Once she had released them, her questions surged on like a craft in swift water. "Are the Shuswaps hostile? Would they massacre settlers? Is someone inciting the Indians?"

After one startled glance, Mrs. Sutherland busied herself over things in a basket. "I think I can take the sting out of this," she said; though she did not make it clear

153

whether she referred to the blood-caked scrapes or to the thoughts that had shocked Megan worse than the tumble. Bathing her injured arm, she began to speak softly of the little girl Alison and the Ross of long ago.

Megan lay back, feeling oddly serene. And as she listened to the tale, her inner turmoil seemed to slacken. It was like emerging from the wild canyon into the broad, placid lower river.

Mrs. Sutherland carried her account up to the time when Mr. MacNeil made financial arrangements for his abandoned family. "Ross and Alison are children of change," she concluded.

"I'm a child of change myself," Megan offered by way of aligning herself with them.

"But not deep change. A child in a close family circle is like a *papoose* laced up snug in his mossbag; he is secure no matter which tree he's hung on."

The drink was taking effect. Yet one question still hovered in the fog. "Why doesn't Mr. Stewart want Ross for Alison? When she's a halfbreed too."

"Megan." The voice was gentle. "I'm a halfbreed, too."

"You?" Megan was dismayed; yet her mind was not clear, somehow. It floated back to Ross and was lost . . . She slept deeply.

She woke with a start. Ross! When he had said *Those raids were reckless, futile things,* he had not been attacking the Company. He had been admitting that he was the raider. At least, the admission meant that the reckless, futile raids were over, as well as that the Company was not the villain. She sighed happily. At least that was settled. Now she had to find a way to make friends with Alison.

Being friends, however, did not seem to have occurred to the Chief Trader's daughter. Next morning, while Megan was being indulged as a convalescent before her mother went back to the dairy, Willie brought in a mid-April issue of *The British Columbian*.

"The riding lady sent it for you, Meg," he announced.

"Well, now!" Mrs. Scully remarked heartily, "If she's not the kind lady!"

There was a marked article, *Execution of the Indians*. Copied from a Minnesota paper, it described the execution of twenty leaders of the 1862 Sioux Massacre. On the morning of the execution, it reported, the Sioux had added fresh streaks of vermilion and ultramarine; they had commenced singing their death song; they had kept on singing it until rifle fire stilled their voices. They had died proud and unrepentent. And then they had all been dumped into a common grave.

She felt sick reading it. These were the Indians who had tortured her friends, thrust live children into stoves. Yet they were also the Indians who had waited for six weeks while their families faced starvation, Indians making a stand for their people.

"You're white as a sheet," Mrs. Scully observed. "Let me see what you're reading. Dear, oh dear, oh dear! No doubt Miss Stewart thought you'd be glad to know that those murdering heathens had been punished."

"Yes, Mama, I guess so." Well, they both had tempers. But this time, Megan owed the apology.

"Mama, I'm going to iron my dress," she announced. According to Willie, Alison had ridden off with her father and Mrs. Sutherland; so Megan had hours to get ready to face the Chief Trader's daughter.

As it turned out, she had days. They had gone to the horse farm. And she waited as patiently as she could, cheered by her release from worry. The camel raids were over. There wouldn't be an Indian rising. Even Mr. Fencil was too busy, she discovered, to promote any mischief.

"Sure, it must be Fencil," Mr. Scully told them after an evening stroll. "They say a tall gink has staked Dowser Claim along a new creek not too far north of us, nowhere near the main diggings."

"Dowser Claim! That's him!" Megan sat up alertly. "Has he found any gold yet?"

"The word is he's found traces."

"See! It works!" All sorts of unexpected things worked. Why, the richest strike of all, Williams Creek, had been located through a dream. Billy Barker, a deserting sailor, had followed a dream, and he had struck gold exactly where the dream had said he would, at fifty-two feet. So you certainly could not scoff at something as sensible as a gold diviner.

Dowser Claim. She envisioned the sign: fancy red lettering and curlycues. Mr. Fencil was clever with his fingers; and he had been so sure of finding gold that he had even planned for a decorative claim stake. She knew because after Mr. Fencil's men had come to the Fort for supplies, she had sneaked a look at the ledger, right away, since names were not put down. On the pretext of studying Mr. Sutherland's beautiful penmanship to see how he wrote *S*, she had looked anxiously to see if Mr. Fencil had sent for much shot and powder, or liquor. He hadn't. He had bought just the usual things: sugar, flour, bacon, beans, tobacco . . . and one little fancy addition. Vermilion. She had sighed with relief. He was obviously concentrating on making a fabulous gold strike.

She could just see him painting *Dowser Claim*. He would get enough gold for a million fancy waistcoats, while the Scullys went on wearing rags.

Alison had not yet returned several nights after the news of Mr. Fencil, when Megan escaped to the river to think of how to move Mama. The scent of willow smoke wafted over the water from campfires on the south bank. She wondered where Connell was. Had he found gold, too? She felt a longing for him.

A squirrel chittered above her. A nighthawk swooped down on a hovering insect. And high in the sky a serene eagle circled above the dark shadows stretching out on the hills.

A shout startled her. At the Fort gate. A horseman raced in.

What on earth had happened? The old chill hit her stomach. She fled to the stockade, where groups of people stood watching the officers' quarters. A lathered cayuse was being rubbed down.

"Come inside!" Mrs. Scully ordered her. "You're shivering."

All her old terrors had come crowding back. She was sick with apprehension by the time her father joined them in the house. She noticed that he lit his pipe with deliberate slowness. Something was the matter! He took infuriatingly long draws to get the thing going well before he turned to speak to them. "There's trouble on the trail," he said quietly. "North this time. Two men have been robbed and murdered."

"Murdered!"

"In a lonely stretch. They were bringing out gold for their Williams Creek partners."

"And . . ." Mrs. Scully demanded.

"And there was a feathered camel sign by the bodies."

"Oh no!" Megan cried out.

"Those murdering heathens!" her mother said, elbows akimbo. "So they're at it again. You're white as a sheet, Meg, and trembling like an aspen. Off to bed, young lady. You're not over that fall yet."

Megan went to bed, glad for a chance to be alone to think. In a way, she might be to blame for this murder. She had infuriated Alison; Alison had thundered off to Ross; and Ross had — No! She refused to think he had done this. Yet he was the camel raider.

Those raids were reckless, futile things. Was it a bitter admission of defeat after all? It could just as well have been a threat of action that was not futile.

Finally she went to sleep only to wake up with a start in the pre-dawn. The camel sign, the one hidden under her ribbons! It was probably the basic pattern and now it was her duty to turn it over to the Police. But how could she ever explain keeping it so long? And what if Ross weren't the camel raider? Or what if he had been, but now it was his Indian cousins who had gone this one fatal step further? If she handed in the sign, he'd get hanged for it.

She tossed in torment, recalling what Mrs. Sutherland had said about his eager childhood. White people had spoiled life for him. Why wouldn't he retaliate?

Yet if the Indians were to rise, if one thing should lead to another, her own little brother might be thrust live into — No! She would not think about it.

11

"Mama," she said first thing in the morning, "about that murder . . ."

"About that murder," her mother murmured with a nod towards Willie in the next room, "we'll have no mention of it this morning."

"No, Mama." Megan sighed. "You know, sometimes I wish I was back in the wagon." It had been good on the trail in spite of the hardships and the everlasting watch for Indians. You might get scared, and dog tired, and dirty, and hungry; but you had no upsetting decisions to make. Only one way was right. Regulations might be irksome; yet they did keep you achieving one more hill, one more river. There was some satisfaction. But here you even had to wonder if people like Ross didn't have the right to drive you and all the other white people out of their country. "Sometimes I do wish I was back on the trail, Mama."

"Well, don't wish me back with you. I've no enthusiasm for rivers without bridges across them. Still, I'll say this for the trail; you weren't cooped up like a hen with a log wall around you. Och, well." Her voice turned wistful. "Once we get to the homestead!"

"It was simpler," Megan remarked, pursuing her own thoughts still.

"Simpler? With no firewood stacked ready to get the pot boiling? And no bed in the mountains till you'd made one of boughs and wet blankets."

"I mean simpler inside you."

Her mother gave her a sharp glance.

"I mean there was only one thing you could do. Just keep pushing ahead."

"Sure it's the same here, Meg. You still just keep pushing ahead."

"If you know which way's ahead."

"You know," her mother said positively. "In a new colony, ahead is whatever way takes you to a home with good acres around you and no war-whoops disturbing the peace. Och, the Indians may have their troubles too," she conceded, "but there's no turning back now for red men or white men. The movement's been started."

That was true. Mama always made sense, except about going to the gold rush. You could no more turn back the white migration than you could turn back a river. That's what she had to tell Miss Alison Stewart after she had handed in the camel sign to the Police. No, before! She would not do what she had to do like *a*

161

silly, vain, stupid, weak, spineless tattletale.

With some apparently innocent queries about Mrs. Sutherland, she learned from Mr. Sutherland that the Chief Trader's party was due back that afternoon.

"Did you call them back because of the murder?"

"The Company's business in May is getting the fur on its way to the ship at Victoria," he answered dryly. "It is not the enforcement of law and order on the colony's trails to the goldfields."

"Of course, Mr. Sutherland." She dashed home; and as soon as the noon dishes were disposed of, she headed for the south bank with Willie and with the ponderosa pine bark camel in the her neatly-ironed pocket.

"Murder," she muttered, reinforcing her resolve. Murder was what she had to remember every time she weakened about informing. And it was that she kept in mind when at last she saw the Chief Trader's party coming.

"Go and watch Papa hammer!" she ordered Willie before she marched briskly to confront Alison.

"Oh . . . Miss Stewart!" she called out.

Alison drew up.

"I haven't had a chance to thank you for saving my life," she said, clearly. Then, when Mr. Stewart and Mrs. Sutherland were farther away, she added fiercely, "There's been a camel sign murder on the Cariboo Trail."

"Murder." Alison appeared to shrivel.

"Get down!" Megan ordered.

Alison dismounted. She seemed stunned.

Megan slid her hand into her pocket and touched the camel sign to fortify her resolve. "Alison," she said gently, "I know that a white feather is a peace sign. And I saw Ross wrench a white feather from his cap and replace it with a red one."

Alison looked surprised.

"And he dropped this from his sash."

The Chief Trader's daughter held herself as still as the pine trees behind her.

Megan heard her own voice become shrill. "It was just raids at first. But now it's robbery and murder." She thrust the sign forward. "And this says Ross did it."

"He didn't. Why would he rob when he has plenty of gold?"

"To keep white men from taking out what he thinks belongs to the natives."

"Ross had nothing to do with this." Alison's voice was positive.

Megan's was as positive. "He did if his raids led his Indian cousins to try robbery and murder." She raised the sign again. "And this says he started the camel raids. This is evidence."

"What are you going to do with your evidence?"

"You know what I have to do."

"Yes, I know, because I heard you give Ross a promise. *Don't be afraid I'll betray you,* you said. *I give you my promise. I'll never betray you.* Remember?"

"Yes, but —"

"But a white girl's promise isn't worth much?"

That did it. Megan's temper exploded. "Look!" she

said. "Obviously the camel raiders want to get rid of white people. So do you! Well I happen to be one of the white people you want to get rid of. Don't forget that I left my last home just before the Sioux massacred my friends. I *know* what can happen when Indians start rising."

"I thought you thought this was Ross, not the Indians?"

"It could be Ross rousing the Indians to drive out the white invaders. And if one murder succeeds, it may mean more will follow. You know that the Indians everywhere are like dry tinder, just waiting for the spark. This says Ross may have provided the spark."

Alison looked at her with horror. "They'd hang him." Her words came out of stark terror. "Judge Begbie would hang him." She shrank back from the sign. "That thing would hang him and he didn't do it."

"Then it wouldn't hang him. You should know that. Haven't you any faith in Judge Begbie?"

"It's not just Judge Begbie. He'd swear in a jury. And you know what he does in these gold cases. He swears in American miners."

"Well?"

"You know what I mean." Alison was almost sobbing. "Men from the American territories. Men used to quick frontier justice. To lynch law. With all that Indian warfare raging in their own territories, you know how they feel about *savages*. Would they trust a halfbreed like Ross? Just on principle, would they?"

Megan lowered her eyes in agreement. "Look Alison,"

she went on gently. "I do realize what could happen to Ross. And I think he's —" She couldn't say that he was like one of the outraged Highland chieftains he had loved to read about, chieftains raiding Lowland farms in righteous indignation. "I think he's heroic, but mistaken. I do know what might happen to him if I turn in the sign. But I also know what might happen to my own little brother if violence spreads through the tribes. I know what can happen."

"Do you?" the other challenged. "Are you sure that getting Ross hanged wouldn't be the spark you were talking about, the spark tossed into dry tinder?"

Megan had to admit she had a point. No matter what you did in this wild Indian country, there was a chance you were wrong. But was it wild Indian country? This was the Crown Colony of British Columbia, where people were bringing their families, where there had to be law. The movement had started and nothing could stop it. People who tried to stop it had to be stopped themselves. "Alison," she said quietly, "I know how you feel about Ross. But there has been a murder. And I have to tell the Police what I know about it. I just simply have to!"

"Yes." Alison agreed in a faint voice. Then she mounted Kalitan and rode on to the canoe landing. Her shoulders stayed square in her beautiful blue broadcloth.

Tears of sympathy blinded Megan. But she did have to inform. She simply had to. And it wouldn't be pleasant for her, either, admitting she had been snooping.

165

She saw the constable's posse go out for him. It was not the posse, however, that brought in the camel raider. It was an Indian party headed by a tall young Shuswap everybody called Tomaah; and it did not stop at Kamloops.

It was dreadful to see Ross a prisoner and to know yourself the informer. Megan could scarcely bear to look.

He sat erect with his hands tied behind him on his lively black stallion. His bonnet still flaunted its angry red feather. And with his proud, Scots bonnet, a brightness seemed to leave the valley.

Megan turned away from the sight to rush into their family quarters. She flung herself on her bed in a torrent of sobbing.

Her mother stroked her hair. "Och, you only did what

167

you had to," she said.

A few minutes later Megan felt Willie's grubby little hand seeking hers. She raised her face to see his troubled blue eyes blinking at her. "Did you *deaded* somebody?" he asked her.

"Oh, I hope not. I hope not!" She sobbed harder than ever. They would hang Ross; and he might not be guilty. All her life she would know that she was the informer. She would see that quick glow on his face and remember what she had done to it. She would never be happy again. Never! No matter how long she lived.

She began avoiding people, especially Alison Stewart. She began to dread reading *The British Columbian*. Rumor had it that Ross had been taken to jail in New Westminster to keep him safely away from his Indian friends and relatives. Nobody knew for sure, though. At least they did not tell her, nor show her the papers that reported his capture.

What somebody did know for sure was the horror of that jail at New Westminster. *A Voice From the Dungeon* spoke in the newspaper:

Startled by the shrieks of a dying maniac on the one hand, and the clanking of the murderer's chains on the other, while the foul and scant atmosphere of our cell, loaded with the noxious affluvia from the filthy dens occupied by lunatics —

She could not bear to read it all. She could only think of Ross in a place like that.

Another issue not only decried the state of the jail; it questioned a man's chance of justice in the colony.

168

There was only one Chief Justice, it reported, with a circuit extending from the Gulf of Georgia to the base of the Rocky Mountains. Men waited in jail for months and months, it claimed; and even then they were not sure of justice.

Mr. Begbie has by recent ruling and decisions on the Bench, most seriously shaken public confidence in, and respect for, our Courts of Justice.

What had she done to Ross? She wished it could all be forgotten. But of course it couldn't be.

One person at least wanted to keep the topic alive, Mr. Fencil! A letter from him appeared in the paper. Alarmed by the raid on himself near Kamloops, he said, and then by the proximity to his claim of the early May camel sign murder, he was circulating a petition for the revival of the Government's armed Gold Escort. *If the British authorities will not permit miners to organize their own armed defense, then they must provide more protection.*

Megan showed it to the family.

"So he's still kicking against the authorities," Mrs. Scully commented.

"But Mama! Don't you agree with him this time?"

"I'd have to know more than I do, which is only that yon scamp's a born agitator."

Agitator? That was true. Maybe he was here for some reason other than gold mining. He had known an awful lot for a newcomer, Megan recalled. *There are big things at stake in the Colony.* Which one was he working for?

She was thankful for the distraction the Fur Brigade offered. For a whole week she was almost too interested to think.

Then another newspaper fell into her hands. With an item cut out! Had Ross been hanged? She could tell nothing from glances at Alison Stewart's face. She could find nothing in the paper. She turned to *News from Cariboo;* though she no longer really cared about the goldrush. Mr. Fencil was there again.

Weeks of patient persistence and faith in his gold diviner are at last paying off for Mr. C. M. Fencil. On May 25th, Dowser Claim washed out 7 pounds 3 ounces. Excitement spread along the creek; but few other traces of gold have so far been found.

That was the way it went. One man struck a pocket of gold from a creekbed affected by some ancient upheaval; while the man next to him found nothing. And it would be Mr. Fencil who was lucky!

"I'm glad that scamp's struck gold," Mrs. Scully remarked. "He'll forget agitating."

"Och, you don't know a thing for sure," Mr. Scully protested mildly. "You're down on the man, Kate."

"I'm down on anybody who might start trouble with the Indians, which is why I'm glad they've clapped that young halfbreed in jail."

"Now don't condemn him too, Kate. Here he's innocent until he's proved guilty. And did it ever occur to you that the camel sign they found at the scene of the murder might have been just a red herring?"

Megan gasped. A red herring, a smell dragged across a trail to wipe out the true scent and draw trackers along a false trail. "Papa!" she cried out in dismay. She had put Ross in jail on the strength of that sign.

"Look at her!" Mrs. Scully said. "White as a sheet again. Merciful Heaven! Once and for all will you stop this talk of the murder!"

"We will, Kate," Mr. Scully agreed. "Especially when we've a gold strike to talk of. So old Fencil's struck gold. I don't mind telling you now I thought yon gink had gone in to salt a few claims and sell them to suckers. Sure I figured that little box he shakes was full of gold for the salting." He told them about men who had salted claims. One had used a shotgun to do it, filling a cartridge with gold dust. Another had secreted tiny nuggets in plugs of chewing tobacco. "And not a soul noticed he hit the pan often, spitting."

"I was suspicious of him too, Papa," Megan said, trying to keep her mind on something besides the camel sign.

"Och, we all were, and we may as well admit we're no judges of human nature."

The next issue she got hold of confirmed the strike at Dowser Claim. So the gold diviner had really worked. Strange, though, Mr. Fencil didn't seem the type for that sort of thing.

Just as Ross didn't seem the kind to commit a murder.

One afternoon she tried to read a book by the river. It was growing unbearably hot. Her clothes stuck to her; and she envied the almost naked children who reveled in mud at the edge of the water. Willie went to sleep with his head in her lap, making her hotter than ever. She leaned back against a tree, and fell asleep also.

She woke like a drowning man surfacing with something. But what? She had caught an idea and then lost it.

When she went to bed that night it was still hovering around like a mosquito. It was something about Mr. Fencil . . . and a red herring.

Red. Red herring. RED! She sat up in bed so suddenly she hit her head on Willie's bunk above her. Red! Mr. Fencil had bought vermilion at Fort Kamloops. Was it to paint the bark and the feathers? He knew what a camel sign looked like because he had been raided; he was clever with his fingers. And he had men who would do a job like murder. Dowser Claim was the red herring! Who would be suspicious of a miner working nearby before and after a murder? A man petitioning for protection! And hadn't she herself reminded him that getting stolen gold OUT of the Cariboo was the big problem? But he could take it out now as his own gold. It was a staggering idea! With men to help him, he could fake a gold strike. But, and here there was a problem, if he was that smart, nobody would ever be able to prove he had faked it. He would have covered all loopholes. And Ross would hang.

There was nothing she could do but clear her mind of Mr. Fencil. She might be right, but she'd never prove it. To put herself to sleep, she tried to think of Connell. A sudden fierce longing for him made her slip out of bed to get the goldpoke he had given her. She put it under her pillow and conjured up that day by the river . . . her embarrassment . . . her joy on discovering he had re-

membered her birthday. She smiled and fell asleep remembering his silly words:

> *The stag at eve had drunk his fill*
> *Where sluiced the maid with her little skill,*
> *Where wild she swirled her goldpan round;*
> *Nor dust, nor flakes, nor nuggets found.*

She woke with a start in the pre-dawn:

> *"You're sure it's a Williams Creek nugget?"*
> *"Look for yourself, Meg. It's blue."*
> *"You mean . . . different gold's different?"*
> *"Certainly. From the different alloys.*
> *Every creek has its special geological conditions.*
> *An expert can tell where a bit of gold came from."*

She felt a deep excitement. Her senses seemed as
acute as an Indian's. There was one little loophole that
even Mr. Fencil's men could not cover. An expert could
tell where a bit of gold came from. They had to get a
sample of that gold before Ross had been hung.

She leaped out of bed, threw her shawl over her nightgown, and slipped out of the house. She flitted through the
moonlight to Alison Stewart's window and hissed through
the mosquito netting.

Alison sat up, startled.

"It's Megan. Maybe we can save Ross."

Alison darted to the window and tore off the netting.
Her face was gaunt in the shadows; and her fingers were

like steel on Megan's shoulders.

Megan tumbled out her tale. Before she had finished, Alison was hauling her through the window.

"Alison, can you send a messenger to the nearest constable?"

"Not a messenger. Us! And not to the nearest constable. To Dowser Claim!"

"But—"

"Look! If we go to the authorities, there will be endless delays. The constable will be fifty miles away. He won't be able to search a man's claim until he has a warrant. And he won't be able to get a warrant until a magistrate gets back from somewhere or other. Don't you know what it's like? They'd delay and delay until it was too late. Until Ross had been hanged. We have to get the sample ourselves."

"But —"

"Do you think they'd hustle themselves for a half-breed agitator?" Alison demanded, almost sobbing.

"Well . . . all right. We'll go." Megan swallowed. She hadn't much choice.

12

"I HAVE OLD RIDING CLOTHES THAT WILL FIT YOU."
Alison tossed garments from a wardrobe.

"But Mama'll —"

"I'll leave a note and Jeannie Sutherland will tell her
something."

Megan snatched up the clothes. She fastened a yellow
bodice above a riding skirt of golden-brown doeskin. And
as she tightened the thong on a Spanish hat, she shivered
with a mixture of pleasure and panic. At last she was
decently dressed. And scared stiff.

Two girls would never get a sample of gold from Mr.
Fencil, especially if it was stolen gold. Yet if no one else
would, they had to. "You're going," she told herself, "and
no poor mouth about it!"

Alison darted in and out. And soon Indians were
opening gates and saddling horses, flitting silently through

the shadows. One sped off.

The girls rode out just before sunup.

"Don't seem to be in a hurry," Alison cautioned as she gathered up Kalitan's reins. She sat straight in her saddle, as patrician as though she were leading the Fur Brigade.

Megan was erect, too; though her stomach was churning.

At first they traveled in almost leisurely quiet. When the sun rose, they swept more freely over rangeland, skirting small lakes and copses of twinkling aspen.

She glimpsed a tipi ahead and a group of Indians with unsaddled cayuses. The word had gone ahead in a hurry.

"This is where we change clothes."

"Change clothes?" Just her luck. She might have known that she'd look nice only briefly.

By the time the girls emerged from the tipi, they were decent Shuswap women in gaudy, shapeless cotton skirts, blouses, and headkerchiefs. Megan's skin had been darkened, her hair hidden. And they were going to the creek to sell beaded moccasins and skin goldpokes, they and a young couple. Megan's eyes lingered regretfully over the lovely riding habit an old squaw was holding.

"We change horses as well," Alison informed her. "Kalitan is too well known. And Megan, from now on we speak not one word of English. Please!"

The couple could not speak English. And they didn't trust a girl who did, Megan decided. She felt their distrust, and avoided their eyes. They blamed her for Ross's condition. But they needed her to identify Mr. Fencil and his men. She clutched that thought to her and stayed close to Alison when they moved off.

Megan and Alison led on buckskin horses. The young squaw, Tukwilla, followed, leading a brown pack mare. Pil Canim, a tall young brave on a piebald, led several spare horses.

They rode fast, on and on and on into sweltering country, a small Indian party with soft-voiced *kla-how-yas* for anyone they encountered. Heedless of heat, they pushed on. And the world grew vaguely unreal. Things swam in Megan's vision: yellowing grass . . . bare bluffs . . . blistering sun . . . The world was hot yellow.

When they finally stopped to make camp at the end of the day, she slid from her horse and her knees buckled under her. She was not used to the trail now. But she made no complaint; and the others ignored her pathetic condition. Perhaps they thought the whole thing was her fault, so she ought to suffer. Perhaps they had brought her along merely to keep her tongue from wagging at Kamloops. Maybe they intended her to fall by the way-side. No! They needed her. They had to get a sample.

She slept for a while. Then wolves woke her. Their desolate howling chilled her blood. Something rustled. A rattlesnake? No matter. Sleep was the important thing. Yet in no time at all, they were shaking her shoulder. They were ordering her onto that terrible cayuse.

It was just as scorching a day as the one before. How could those others travel and travel and travel, and never seem weary?

Suddenly, Alison was alert. She glanced back.

"K'lahma!" she muttered, and spurred off across country to draw him away from the Indians, who instantly thundered forward.

Instinctively Megan wheeled to follow the Chief Trader's daughter. Alison was her safety: Alison and K'lahma, who would force them to go home.

She checked her gallop. There was no turning back now. She had a job to finish. She wheeled again, to race after the Indians.

Kicking the buckskin mercilessly, she closed the gap between herself and Pil Canim. The Indians wouldn't harm her while they needed her. They wouldn't!

After that they traveled warily but fast. And they camped warily and briefly in a beautiful pinewood carpeted by wild flowers. Surprisingly, Megan found herself relaxing. Tukwilla and Pil Canim enjoyed little jokes together; they regarded each other fondly. They were just people! Not quiet, subdued people like the Indian wives at Fort Kamloops. These two were lively people!

Next afternoon they moved off the lonely trails they had been following onto the Cariboo Wagon Road. And when a light wagon passed them and the whip-cracking driver made lewd remarks to her, Megan flushed and kept her head low. She must really look like an Indian to be treated so rudely! A bullock wagon creaked by. Two horsemen passed southward.

Then there was a long, long lonely stretch before they turned off, along a creek.

"Dowser?" She scarcely breathed it; yet Tukwilla nodded.

Megan's mouth went dry. She felt her last ounce of courage ooze out. Here they were, riding towards a man who could teach a fox how to be tricky; who would be as alert as a fox, too; who might even recognize her in spite of the skin dye. Her heart thumped. If she ever did get out of this alive, she would settle down gladly to baking and scrubbing. She would mind her own business forever and ever.

She swallowed her panic as best she could as they moved along the creek, past three prospectors. Rounding a stand of cottonwood, she saw him, near a sluicebox. There was his sign, all fancy red lettering and curlycues, and his two men.

His eyes narrowed as he saw the approaching Indian party. His hand jiggled something.

Tukwilla evidently caught her start, and made happy noises and pointed towards a spot for the tipi.

Megan kept her head down as she rode on past the men. She was trembling like an aspen. "You're sixteen," she told herself fiercely, "and this time you had better act like it!" There were no palisades now. When she had wheeled back from Alison, she had discarded safety.

Her companions were a picture of unconcern. Pil Canim watered the horses. Tukwilla unlashed lodgepoles. And not until they were pleasantly settled did they give her orders, apparently about the campfire, and approach Dowser Claim with their beautifully beaded items.

Sneaking furtive glances as she gathered firewood, Megan thought Mr. Fencil was upset. His men moved closer to him. Men guarding gold had itchy trigger-

179

fingers; and men who had deliberately thrown guilt on Indians, would be wary of Indians. She swallowed. And so there was no chance that he would not be suspicious of them, ready for whatever move they might make.

Nevertheless Pil Canim stood calmly with his arms crossed while Tukwilla displayed skinwares.

Mr. Fencil and his men were buying! Soon they would pay with gold dust and the job would be finished. Megan almost held her breath, waiting; and she sagged with relief when Mr. Fencil finally put his hand into his pocket.

He pulled out a banknote.

Pil Canim shook his head. "Pil Chickimin." Gold.

Instantly two big hands spread and waited above two guns. Megan's heart thudded in her ribcage.

The small box shiggled. And then, as though on sudden, happy impulse, Mr. Fencil held the box towards the Indian. "Pil Chickimin," he agreed, opening it to show that it contained gold.

But that gold could have come into the country with him.

Megan lacked Shuswap words to explain to the couple when they came back. She tried to pantomime her concern; and though they glanced at her sharply, they went on flashing the brass box with primitive delight in a strange, new, bright treasure.

It worried her. Mr. Fencil was not given to generous impulses. She watched when she could. Once, she saw the men uncover a packsaddle. They were moving out! She nudged Tukwilla.

Still the Indians appeared unconcerned. Couldn't they understand? She tried to eat a little. Later she tried to sleep a little. And this time it was not fear of Indians that made her creep out at sunup.

The white men were certainly striking camp.

So were the Indians, and not without an attempt to sell one of the spare horses to Mr. Fencil. Maybe they did understand. She found herself sweating before the heat of the day had even started.

Since the Indian party followed the white men out to the road, Megan heard Mr. Fencil tell the three prospectors that Dowser Claim was played out. "It was one of those pockets." He gave them each a banknote "for luck!" and advised them to move north to the main diggings. He'd have friendly witnesses, if it came to a showdown.

When they had reached the road, they followed him southward. This morning it was deserted. Only one group of horsemen passed them, going north to the richer gold-fields.

It was terribly lonely, with some dark stands of timber. But she just would not panic. He wouldn't shoot them, she reminded herself firmly. All he could be today was a respectable miner taking his gold out. He knew that; no holsters were visible. Just rifles. If he thought he was in the presence of thieves, of course, he could take measures.

A hunch grew in Megan. Mr. Fencil must suspect. He was going to do something.

She almost cheered when a flash of red came round a bend up ahead. Soldiers! The Royal Engineers who were pushing the road through! Had Mr. Fencil known they were here? She didn't care what Pil Canim might have planned. He didn't know Mr. Tricky Fencil. She did. She was not taking any more chances. The minute she was within earshot, she was going to yell and spur forward.

But things started happening before she could.

One of the men cantered back behind the Indians, leveling a rifle at them. The other took his place ahead of them, leveling his gun also. Surrounding them!

The Engineers came on. Sappers sat in the wagon; non-commissioned officers moved as outriders. And up ahead rode the officer, tall and commanding. With him, on a mettlesome black, rode a man dressed like a Chief Trader.

Not until Mr. Fencil had hailed the soldiers did his plan come clear to her. He was making a citizen's arrest. He was pretending that he had captured criminals. His audacity stunned her. He was going to play the righteous gold miner defending his property now that the Gold Escort had been disbanded.

What Mr. Tricky Fencil did not know was that he had captured a white girl, a girl who could talk just as glibly as he could.

She felt the rifle nudge her forward, and she swallowed her panic again. He'd be quick as a snake if he needed to shoot her, and he'd be clever enough to find a good reason for it. She must not hurry or bungle things. She must wait for the right moment. She hung her head and stayed silent.

The Captain alerted his troop with a clipped command. He halted his Engineers with a lift of his gloved hand.

Mr. Fencil greeted him with apparent relief. "You have come along most opportunely, sir. Most opportunely! I believe it's in order to call upon the military in a civil emergency?"

That man knew everything! Except one little thing, that he had captured a white girl. She watched him covertly. And she had difficulty controlling some indignant snorts at the story he told:

These Indians were thieves. They had already stolen a treasured keepsake of his, a small brass box filled with the first gold dust he had ever mined. But what really alarmed him was the possibility that these Indians were scouts for the notorious camel raider's gang. He had suffered through one of their raids on his way into the country; he had lived in fear of another at Dowser Claim. He had appealed in vain to the Government to revive the Gold Escort. It was truly providential, this arrival of the soldiers. He begged the Captain to take charge of the thieves. He demanded an armed escort. "There has already been a robbery and murder in this very region," he concluded ringingly. "Prevent a second one, sir!"

The officer had listened in disciplined silence. Not until Mr. Fencil had finished did he turn to his companion. "Mr. Fitzgerald," he said, as though presenting the problem to the man who could properly deal with it.

Mr. Fitzgerald! This must be Judge Fitzgerald, as the miners called him. A gold commissioner, and so a magistrate as well.

"This isn't my district, Captain," the magistrate protested.

Megan stiffened. Just as Alison had said: delays . . . warrants . . . legal balderdash while a boy was being hanged! Her involuntary start brought a nudge from the rifle.

It was Mr. Fencil who challenged the magistrate's protest. "Surely, Judge Fitzgerald, one needn't be too meticulous in a wilderness where Indians are raiding and robbing and murdering. After all, it's the Queen's Peace that matters and not small legal quibbles. There has been one camel sign murder here, sir. I beg you to prevent another." He looked suitably distraught.

The Captain sat awaiting the magistrate's decision. Obviously the military could not interfere in civil affairs

unless called upon to do so by the proper authorities.
Alison had been right; and Megan did not dare chance
things. If they shot her, they shot her. "Help me!" she
yelled, yanking off her kerchief. "I'm white. Help me!"

At least she forced action.

"Arrest the whole party!"

Men barked out commands. Rifles came up. A ring
of steel was flung around all the travelers.

"Take charge of that girl!" she heard the Captain
command; and she was promptly led to him.

"Well!" Mr. Fencil exclaimed; and his surprise was
one thing he did not need to fake. "If it isn't Miss Wagon
Train again, got up in paint and feathers!" He turned to
the others, his voice sad but indulgent. "It's Megan Scully
from Kamloops. You'll have to forgive her, poor thing.

She was one of the overlanders. I'm sure you'll understand, Captain, Judge Fitzgerald. After that trek through the Rockies, even white men became cannibals." He whispered the awful word. "It was too much for a highly-strung white girl." He looked at her, solicitous but accusing. "Still, Megan dear! Taking up with thieves!"

"They're not thieves! You're the thief!"

"So that's it." He seemed very relieved, though he shook his head sadly as he turned back to the others. "I'm afraid little Megan does have an obsession. She told me about it herself when I came in through Kamloops. She is going to capture a gunman and win a reward for a grubstake for her father. Wasn't that what you said, dear?"

She felt her face reddening. She glared at him, then ignored him. "Judge Fitzgerald," she pleaded, "these Indians are not thieves. They sold Mr. Fencil moccasins and goldpokes; and he paid them with the brass box. And I know why!" She scowled triumphantly at the villain.

Everybody looked at her.

"I would have stolen, though, if you must know," she went on, "to get a sample of that gold you were mining, Mr. Fencil."

"A sample of the gold?" Mr. Fitzgerald's soft voice betrayed no urgent interest.

"It might be the gold that was stolen in the camel sign robbery, sir."

"My poor, dear Megan," Mr. Fencil broke in gently, "you really must not give way to this obsession. I'll give your Papa a grubstake myself, dear, for old times sake."

Full of concern for the plight of the addled darling, he appealed to the magistrate. "Don't you think it's our duty to get this poor child home to her parents? I withdraw my complaints, of course. I wouldn't dream of pressing charges. Sorry to have detained you, Judge Fitzgerald, Captain." He lifted his hat with deference.

"Please!" Megan said desperately. "It might be the stolen gold!"

Mr. Fencil continued soothingly. "Megan dear, that robbery was part of a native rebellion. The renegade halfbreed leader was captured red-handed."

"Ross didn't do it!" She knew she was screeching; she was proving his lies by hysterical conduct. "Judge Fitzgerald," she said, controlling her voice, "won't you please take a look at his gold, sir? Won't you see if it's Williams Creek gold?"

"Hysteria," Mr. Fencil commented; though as if his long patience was nearing its end.

The gold commissioner's reply was pleasantly placating. "Don't you think we might humor the girl, Mr. Fencil, a high-strung girl with a dangerous obsession?" He held out his hand for a sample.

Mr. Fencil protested. "It's most carefully packed away, sir."

"Still, I'm afraid I insist, since our first concern is for this poor child, isn't it?"

"I'm afraid I insist also, Mr. Fitzgerald. As you said, this is not your district. And I have withdrawn all charges."

"But as you said, Mr. Fencil, one needn't be too

meticulous in the wilderness. I choose to humor the poor girl. So, a sample of your gold if you please, sir."

The Captain betrayed no emotion whatever. He could have been an equestrian statue.

Mr. Fencil and his men produced a goldpoke with obvious reluctance, such obvious reluctance that the commissioner remarked, "Have no fear for your gold, Mr. Fencil. Government pay is not all that bad, in spite of what the papers say." He poured a dribble on his palm.

Was it blue?

He glanced at it only casually before dribbling it carefully back into the goldpoke. "Where did this gold come from?" he asked, as if filling out a boring legal form.

"From my registered claim, sir. It's all perfectly legal." Then, as though joking, he added, "Which is more than I can say for your worship's actions: illegal arrest . . . no jurisdiction . . . no search warrant . . . and no hard feelings, Judge Fitzgerald," he added as he smilingly held out his hand for the goldpoke.

The Commissioner smiled back at him. "Since you do like to be legal, Mr. Fencil, we'll let you sign a statement; and we'll give you a receipt for this gold, which I'll keep for the time being." He turned to the Captain. "Shall we move to a better halting place, Captain? There was an area just back of that bend, I noticed."

At the better halting place, a sapper made tea; and Megan signed a statement. "Please hurry about the gold!" she begged. "Please don't let Ross be hanged before they find out if he's guilty!" She fervently hoped that two riders dispatched southward were bound for New West-

188

minster to stay proceedings.

Suddenly she had a new idea. Maybe they would all be taken to New Westminster; there'd be a big, important trial with Judge Begbie in his wig. She would go on the stand. She envisioned herself in the new dress Mama would get, not to let her disgrace the family. Yellow! No. Quiet blue for a trial. She could just see Ross in that jaunty Scots bonnet; she could see the glow on his face when he heard how she had saved him. Megan sipped her tea with a dignity befitting a young lady whose name would appear in *The British Columbian*. Connell, wherever he was, would read all about it.

"And now, Miss Megan," Mr. Fitzgerald was saying, "you are going home."

"Home? But I'm arrested like everyone else." She was not going to be packed off home like a child before anything was settled. "Please sir, I'm very involved in this. You don't know all I've done."

"What you have done, child, is run away from home. You are going home, now."

"Yes, sir." She would not make a poor mouth about it. She'd look pleasant if it killed her.

"Arrested!" Mrs. Scully said for the ninth or fifteenth time. "My daughter! Arrested!"

"Did you nearly get deaded?" asked Willie.

"She did," said his mother. "And us thinking she was safe with the Chief Trader's daughter! We'd have worried to death if we'd known. Och, Meg! Why didn't you tell us?"

189

"You'd have worried to death," Megan answered demurely. "But why worry now, Mama, when the danger's all over?"

"Oh, it's all over, is it?" Mrs. Scully said. "You went flying off on a cloud of supposings: Suppose Mr. Fencil stole the gold. Suppose he planted the camel sign as a red herring. Suppose he faked a gold strike . . . Well! Suppose you listen to me for a minute, young lady, while I give you a bit of supposing to put in your pipe! Suppose Mr. Fencil's gold has come out of Dowser Claim after all. Suppose he's turned loose by Judge Fitzgerald. And suppose he's annoyed by the trouble you've caused him. Suppose your Indian friends are locked up as thieves. And suppose their Indian friends blame the white people for it. Suppose —" She grabbed the girl fiercely to hug and protect her. "Suppose you'd been killed, Meg!"

"Suppose we all get deaded," said Willie, looking worried.

"Och, suppose we all have a nice cup of tea and forget all about it." Mrs. Scully's brisk spirits rose once more. "Arrested! My daughter! And me thinking she was safe with the Chief Trader's daughter."

"Mama, you're sure she hasn't come back?"

"I've not clapped my eyes on her."

"Neither me," asserted Wilie. "I seed Mr. Stewart go away, and Mrs. Sutherland."

Where on earth was Alison? And what was happening? What would happen? Mama did make sense, usually; and it had all been supposings. Perhaps she had caused nothing but more trouble. Why did she always give way to an impulse?

No, she didn't always. Once, when K'lahma had appeared, she had not rushed, terrified, to safety. She had deliberately turned back and followed the Indians. And, come to think of it, there had been a new look in their eyes after that. On that occasion she had acted like sixteen. For once in her life, she had acted like sixteen.

13

July was hot at Kamloops. Hot and endless!

How brown the hills had become, Megan thought late one afternoon. They shaded from the pale glistening gold of dried grass to the dark brown of draws running back from the river. If you half closed your eyes, the shadows were folds in the skin of great, tawny beasts who crouched there in the sunshine, waiting.

Why wasn't there some word of Alison? Ross? Mr. Fencil? Connell!

The scorching breeze itself seemed to carry in news about everything else. The Royal Engineers were disbanding. Governor Douglas was going to be knighted. Smallpox had broken out again in the Indian encampments. The Chilcotin Indians were alarmingly restless, west of the Fraser River. Fabulous gold strikes were still being made in the Cariboo diggings; in Stout's Gulch, they said, every man was a Midas. There was soon going to be a stagecoach running into the goldfields, like California.

"More of our overlanders have struck it rich," Mr. Scully reported one sweltering evening. "Do you mind the two Watties, Kate? Well, they're taking out a hundred and fifty ounces of gold every twenty-four hours."

"Oh, Papa!" Megan's pleasure was tinged with envy.

"Maybe it would have been wise after all, Kate, to just pick up and go. To get a good stake for that homestead you're wanting."

"A good stake if you're lucky," she retorted, "and a good, plain, pine box if the luck goes against you. Och, there's many a man getting nothing but blisters, and holes in his britches while his children grow thin on just hope and potatoes."

Megan knew now that they'd never go to the diggings. They'd stay here at Fort Kamloops for ever and ever and wizen up in the sun.

She hated the sun.

She hated Fort Kamloops.

She hated her drab washed-out dresses. Though what did it matter how she looked? Connell would never come back.

She hated *The British Columbian*. It took ten million years to find out about something, and then ten million more to get up to Fort Kamloops. Lately it had not arrived at all, unless someone was deliberately keeping it from her.

And where was everybody? Probably at the trial;

while she sat here, ignored, as if she had had nothing to do with the matter.

Then one afternoon she saw K'lahma coming in from the West. Her heart leaped at the prospect of news, but her stomach went cold with forebodings. What if Ross had been hanged?

All of a sudden she didn't want to know. Yet it was infuriating to have the Fort swallow K'lahma in absolute silence.

She could not eat her supper. She could not bear to stay in the house. And she simply could not stand the confinement of the compound.

When she slipped out through the gate, she saw a large party approaching from the west on the north bank. Even at a distance, she recognized the Chief Trader and his daughter. Had they come from north of the river? Or had they come from New Westminster and crossed the Thompson below Lake Kamloops?

With news so close, she felt sick. What if Ross had been hanged? She just could not face it. So she went down to the river, to her favorite ponderosa. She'd stay there, leaning against the tree, watching the sun set.

As always, the valley was lovely at sunset. Rosy mauve tints deepened into purple. It was almost overwhelming, but Megan had no mind for it. She felt worse by the minute; but she would not let the tears come. She leaned against the pine tree, refusing to cry, and waited.

"Kla-how-ya!"

She whirled round, her face lighting with joy. That was a welcome voice. "Connell! Oh, Connell!" He stood

tall and suntanned, his eyes bluer than ever above his neckerchief.

"Meg!" He caught both her hands.

"Oh, Connell! I guess I didn't really expect you. I thought you'd gone forever." She'd forgotten how blue his eyes were. "Were you in the Chief Trader's party?"

"Just behind it."

"Have they brought any word?" She simply had to ask it.

"About . . . ?" His word dared her to ask further.

"About Ross."

His hand dropped hers.

"He won't hang." The news appeared to give him no particular pleasure. Then he grabbed her shoulders. "Meg, why did you do it? Why did you risk your neck going after a scoundrel like Fencil?" He shook her. "Oh, I've read all about you, you brave little white girl. You absolute *looney!* Meg, why did you do it?"

Aghast at his fury, she just stared at him.

"Risking your neck for a renegade halfbreed!"

That angered her.

"Why? Can't you guess? To get a reward for a grub-stake." It was a new idea, but an interesting one.

"Tell me the truth!" He was hurting her shoulders. "Why did you do it?"

She answered quietly, looking straight up at him. "I did it to save Ross from hanging."

He dropped his arms and gazed off over the river until the sound of a horse approaching made both of them glance round.

"Alison!" Megan darted forward.

Alison reined in and dismounted. "It was Mr. Fencil as you suspected," she said. "I came to thank you and . . . and, Oh Megan! I was terrible to you."

She was so wan! As forlorn as a lost child. Megan went to her, arms wide. And the girls clung together, Alison sobbing.

"Alison. Alison," Megan said, soothing her. "It's all over now. He'll be free. He'll be back at Kamloops."

A fresh burst of sobbing answered.

"Can't you tell me what's happened?" Megan begged.

"He disappeared. He's probably angry about being in jail. Maybe he'll —" She could not say what he might do.

The two girls drew apart as they heard another horse coming down the path.

"It's K'lahma," Megan whispered.

Alison controlled her sobs. "Checking to see that I don't disappear, too, I suppose."

Megan dabbed at Alison's face with her handkerchief. She straightened the Spanish hat. "I'll come and talk to you later," she promised softly. "Come on, Chief Trader's daughter!" She smiled hearteningly as Alison regained her composure. But her gray eyes misted as she watched the other mount Kalitan and settle herself into haughty erectness. "I love Alison Stewart," she found herself saying.

She felt a quick arm round her shoulders.

"You love Alison Stewart," a deep voice agreed. "But how do you feel about Connell Moore?"

She glanced up to find his eyes blue and repentent;

197

and she lowered her own. Then she lifted her chin. She was going to act like sixteen again, if it killed her. "I feel the way I've always felt about him," she said distinctly. "Why do you think I've kept wanting to go to the diggings? Just . . . Just to have pretty dresses so you'd finally see me." There! The admission was out. He could think what he would think.

"Pretty dresses?" He hooted. Then he grabbed her and hugged her. "So I'd see you, Megan! Do you know what I see every night? Every morning? I see the way your face lights when I come suddenly on you. That's what I see, Meg. The way your face lights up."

"Proving Mama knows best," she answered. "Och," she mimicked Kate Scully. "The most important thing any girl wears is the look on her face."

Connell laughed with her before he turned serious. "Riding towards Kamloops today, I kept wondering if it would light up for me this time. I was afraid that maybe you —" He dismissed his foolish fear. "You can't know how I need to be sure of your welcome."

Sheer surprise filled her eyes. A rush of tenderness went through her. She laid a hand on his cheek and felt him lean swiftly against it. "Why didn't you say so before?" she demanded. "Why didn't you say something when you came here last time?"

"Well, you seemed so . . ."

"I know." Childish! So encircled by vanities and thoughts of herself that she hadn't been able to see out. She had thought he wasn't seeing her; when all the time she hadn't been seeing him. She hadn't seen his needs, nor Alison's, nor anybody's. Well, now she was sixteen. "Did you spot any good land, Connell?" she asked out of her sudden wisdom.

The glow on his face was quick proof of that wisdom. "You've never seen anything like it, Meg. Beautiful grass and trees. Good water. Close to the markets. My family likes the sound of it."

"Your family!" She had forgotten his family. Gentry who might not like the sound of Megan Scully.

"Maddest people you ever saw," he conceded, misinterpreting her look. "But then you're none too sensible yourself, Meg. You'll likely take to them. My maddest brother's on his way now."

They laughed together. "All it needs is a little work . . . and someone whose face will light up when I ride in for dinner."

"Is that a fact, Connell?" She couldn't help teasing him. "But you wouldn't be wanting an absolute *looney*."

"I might, since there isn't much choice in gold-mining country." He grinned at her. "Still, there is one small matter."

She was alarmed in spite of herself.

"This is gold mining country," he reminded her, "and before a man stakes a claim he does prospect a little, just to make sure there's pay dirt."

"Could I get you a goldpan?"

That was all she had a chance to say.

"Did . . . you find any color?" Megan asked him when she had caught her breath.

"A bonanza! Can I stake the claim, Megan?"

"Well . . ." She appeared to consider. "I suppose it is time someone was staking something after crossing those plains and those mountains to get here."

"You'll love the ranch," he promised. Then he frowned.

"But . . . what, Connell?"

"Oh . . ." He shrugged. "Indians are —"

"Indians!" She didn't mean it to be loud.

He was indulgent, but impatient. "Aren't you over that Sioux fright yet? You know the Indians here are friendly."

"Are they claiming your land?" she asked him anxiously.

"Just one corner. You know how they are. They don't use half the land the Government allots them; yet they won't give it up to someone who will use it. But don't trouble your head. We've good courts here, Meg. What's the matter?"

"Connell. We don't need their corner."

He was surprised, but still tolerant. "All right, Meg. I understand."

"I'm not sure you do." She scarcely did herself. It was not fear. Fear, like vanity, kept you from seeing much and she seemed to understand things now as she hadn't before.

"Meg, your mind's racing away again," Connell accused her.

"I'm sorry, but I simply cannot keep my mind off Ross. Indians, and Indian problems remind me of him. He disappeared. Where can he be, Connell?"

"I hope we don't find out by a raid on the gold trails."

Megan swallowed.

He wouldn't start raiding again!

Would he?

14

ALISON STEWART, EVEN MORE THAN MEGAN, COULD not keep her thoughts off Ross. Where was he? What had happened to him? Day after day she had waited for some kind of word. Surely he had not gone off on some other foolish errand. It was one thing to be really Indian, and another to be foolishly defiant about it. She could see that now.

Her patience was almost at an end, and she would have ridden off herself to find him, if, amazingly, he hadn't ridden into the post himself. He was not alone. A number of Indians from the camel raid area, one of them the old chief, Red Feather's grandfather, were with him.

Alison saw them coming from a distance. And for one awful moment she thought the Indians were bringing him in again as a prisoner for the old camel raid charges.

Then, when she saw more closely, it was his clear sense of freedom that alarmed her. What had so lifted his spirits? He had never seemed so good-looking, so dashing in his jaunty Scots bonnet! So heart-breakingly endearing! What had he done now? What else was he planning?

Her father came out and there were the usual courtesies to the old chief. Ross was being very formal. She could hardly bear it. Then she caught his glance, and that was all she needed. In that one exchange, everything was said that needed to be said.

Quietly she followed the delegation into the formal trading room. The chief had indicated he had many things to say. She hoped her father would not see her and ask her to leave. He still did not believe that women should be a part of business dealings, even when they were so intimately concerned.

It soon became clear that the old chief was not asking that Ross be cleared by the white men of the old camel charges against him. The chief was stating that the white men had no jurisdiction over the Indians. There was no treaty. As far as the Indians were concerned, Ross was a free man. The Queen's peace had no basis in their eyes, nor white man's justice.

Her father looked on as the old man had his say. Mr. Stewart's face was stern and closed. Even Alison could not tell what he was thinking.

Dismissing Ross's problem as closed, the old chief went on, "Four time four years ago, the great brigades of our friends no longer came through our valley. Settler," he spat the word out, "had reached the hunting grounds of our neighbors to the south. The Cayuse War had started. It was no longer safe for our friends to take the great brigades south to the river white men called the Columbia. My people met at Fort Colvile in Council. We knew that one day settlers would come to our valley, too. We knew that bloodshed would come with them. To prevent that, we presented our valley to a friend."

"Angus McDonald, chief trader then at Fort Colvile," Mr. Stewart murmured in acknowledgment.

"Our friend has not yet claimed our valley. Yet it is still ours to protect for him. And that is what I am here to tell you we will do. We do not want to have our valley become the Valley of the Camels. We know that the owner of the camels and others have asked for land grants there. But our valley is not the Queen's to grant. I am telling this to you, and I will send word to the Governor; he is the true friend of Indians, as I believe you are. We will protect our land, and we will expect you to do the same." The old chief's proud eyes flashed. There was no humiliation in his bearing. He knew, as Alison did now, that it was not what people did to you, but what you were willing to accept from them that shamed you.

Mr. Stewart said little in reply, except that he would do what he could. There was little ground for hope in his words that the Indians would win in the end.

At last, the ceremonies concluded, the chief and the Indians with him turned to leave. Alison did not know quite what to expect from Ross, but she did not think he would leave. And she was right.

It was after the Indians had gone that he caught her hand and followed her father into the Chief Trader's parlor. For the first time that afternoon, her father looked really angry.

"There was no need to make this dramatic Indian stand, Ross," the Chief Trader said coolly. "You might have known we would do what we could for you. I went to the Governor myself to get your pardon for those foolish camel raids. And I assured Mr. Douglas that the Company needed you for the brigades and that there would be no more trouble. There was no need for you to rouse the Indians."

"There was no need for me to rouse the Indians, sir," Ross agreed quietly. "The land grants to settlers had already done that, and the miserable reserves. I went to the valley intending to give myself up there, assuming that I was wanted in that district for those old camel raids. I didn't want another long march as a prisoner. But the old chief wouldn't let me give myself up. He insisted on coming here. I appreciate what you did for me, Mr. Stewart. And I'll make good your word to Mr. Douglas. I'll see the outfits through to Alexandria and the horses to the winter ranges. Then . . ." He drew Alison's arm through his.

She lifted her head, high. "Then he's going to marry me, Father."

"Not without my consent, Alison. You are not going to live like an Indian."

"Why not?" She was an Indian.

Ross intervened gently. "Not even a full-blooded Indian can live like an Indian any longer, Mr. Stewart. But don't worry about Alison. I have gold, at least."

"That's the point, Ross. You have gold. You could make something of yourself in the Colony. You could set up as a rancher; you've always had a way with horses. But you must forget the past. You must accept change. You've seen the Company accept it. Aren't we tearing down the palisades here? Accept a fact, Ross! This is not Indian territory now."

"No, it is not!" Ross agreed, "though there's no treaty that says so."

"Don't be a hot head about Indians. It could ruin your future. Indians will have to accept change, too."

"In the form of inadequate parcels of land, sir?"

"Be reasonable, lad! They don't use half the land they've been allotted."

"You mean they don't plow it. I might have expected my father to say that, but not you, Mr. Stewart."

That hit, Alison noticed. Her father's voice was softer when he next spoke.

"They could run cattle like Lolo."

"Enough cattle for the whole Kamloops Band, for instance, on the two narrow strips they have been allotted?"

"Look! Any man in that Band could have more land and you know it. All he has to do is get out and pre-empt it, like a white man."

"And prove up on it, like a white man," Ross added. "Build a squared-log house with a shingled roof, cultivate a white man's turnip patch. Why should he have to become a white man to qualify for land in his own country?"

"Ross, I know that a white man did not treat you well; and as a white man, I'm sorry. But an Indian did not treat you well, either. It was your old Indian friend, Tomaah, who betrayed your whereabouts, when you were wanted for murder."

"My old Indian friend Tomaah was corrupted in his childhood. Djaada knew that."

"Djaada?"

"What do you think broke your wife's heart, Mr. Stewart?"

"I know what broke her heart. What had been done to her people."

"No."

Mr. Stewart looked startled.

"What broke Djaada's heart was what was done by her people. They accepted degradation."

"That's true, Father," Alison broke in. "You know that whatever else, no matter how unhappy or lonely she was, she kept her dignity. It was the one thing she could not bear to lose, and the one thing the Indians could have kept, if they had tried."

Mr. Stewart glanced at her in such surprise that she suddenly realized he had never thought of Djaada as lonely or unhappy.

"You didn't know?" she said lamely. "She was desperately lonely for her own kind of people. For fun and laughter, Indian fun and laughter."

"Your mother never complained."

"Well, she should have. Don't you understand, Father? Indians, and halfbreeds, shouldn't just accept the white man's way when it makes them grow desperate inside themselves. They should find their own way of living. It's one thing to accept change, but another to have to make yourself into something you're not. To be himself, that's all Ross wants, Father."

"Then that's what Ross had better go after. But for you, I want a good life."

"I know you do, Father." She hated to upset him. "You want me to live in a mansion in Victoria and wear billowing silk dresses and eat my heart out."

"Why should you eat your heart out? What's wrong with a good life?"

"That's what we're asking you, Father. What's wrong with a good life? The kind of life that will make you happy, that's right for you."

"I see," he answered bleakly. "I'll save my breath to cool my porridge."

Ross tried reason. "It's a matter of values, Mr. Stewart. As long as I can remember, there's been only one standard of value, a prime beaver. Everything else had to be *Made Beaver* to have its value. A knife was two *Made Beaver,* a gun twenty, but the standard of value has changed already. You said I have to accept change, sir. Perhaps you have to accept it also."

"Certain standards are basic," the man countered. "Which reminds me. Your father is arriving. He's coming back for his keepsakes." He indicated the portrait. "I suppose you won't want to meet him."

"Why not, sir? It's not what people do to you that shames you. It's only what you do that shames you."

"And what we do," Alison broke in again, "is respect custom-of-the-country marriage. Ross claims the MacNeil name. And so will I."

"What you claim is neither here nor there," her father informed her. "This is a British Colony, with British marriage requirements. Very well! When your father arrives, there will be a belated adoption ceremony, conducted by me, in private. Your name is going to be legal, whether you care or not, Ross."

Alison relaxed. It would be all right. They just had to be patient. They mustn't push him too far too fast.

"Father!" she exclaimed, as though suddenly remembering something, when in truth she was just making it up. "We can't talk any more now. I have social duties to attend to."

He glanced at her in surprise.

"Megan Scully risked her life for law and order. And she deserves something from me, from both of us, especially since she's engaged, too."

"To the young Irish gentleman?" Mr. Stewart smiled.

"We're going to entertain them this evening. Ross and I should get to know a white couple."

"Aye." Mr. Stewart looked brighter than he had in a long time.

"So, if you'll excuse us, Father, I have things to do."

Her father was not listening. "You say your mother was unhappy."

"Just when she was lonely." She looked pleadingly at him. "I don't want to be as lonely, Father."

"Away with you and plan your evening." He dismissed her with a gesture, his thoughts still on Djaada.

"Ross," Alison said when they were alone. "It's all going to work out right."

"It is, Highborn Lady." His strong arms went round her.

It wasn't all going to work out right. They both knew that. But they would live by their values.

They clung fiercely together.

Next morning Megan was near the corral with her family when Alison and Ross rode out. She caught his words: *She is won. We are gone, over bank, bush, and scar.*

"Good luck, Young Lochinvar," she called softly. She turned starry eyes on her mother. "Isn't it wonderful, Mama!"

"It's wonderful they don't break their necks, the way those two ride. They've wild streaks, both of them. They're born rebels."

"Then wouldn't it be worse if they weren't together?" Mr. Scully demanded. "If there's one thing a rebel needs, it's another to keep him in order."

"Up the rebels!" said Megan. She had never dreamed of such a friend as the Chief Trader's daughter.